T0064416

DESTINY

DESTINY

TANGIR TABI

PARTRIDGE
A Penguin Random House Company

ISBN: Softcover   978-1-4828-5913-3
               eBook   978-1-4828-5914-0

Print information available on the last page.

To order additional copies of this book, contact
Partridge India
000 800 10062 62
orders.india@partridgepublishing.com

www.partridgepublishing.com/india

CONTENTS

ACKNOWLEDGEMENTS

First of all, I would like to thank God for giving me the power of creativity. My dear wife, Agam Ete Tabi for constant support and encouragements. Thanks to my elder sister Oyang Tabi Pada, who has always been there through thick and thin.

Thanks to my life long friend Micky. He is the first reader of my manuscript, who came up with valuable suggestions. Special thanks to my friend Tunge Lollen, Assistant Professor, Donyi Polo Kamki College for proof reading and appreciation.

Huge thanks to my brother Er. Adi Tabi, for moral support and enthusiasm in my work. Without him my dream of publishing wouldn't have been materialised. Thanks to the publishing team of Partridge India.

DEDICATED TO

My wife Agam Ete Tabi

And

My elder sister Oyang Tabi Pada

FEW WORDS TO SHARE

The present work is my first venture without any specific motives behind. It's just a work of my mind and creation at large, and an expression of a hobby. It's the result of my long jotting and scrabbling habit since my school days. The characters in the story are fictious and some of the places, events and incidents or locales are entirely coincidental.

Readers' comments and critiscism are highly welcomed, which would encourage me to come up with yet another stories to entice you in the future.

TANGIR TABI

CHAPTER ONE

THE EARLY YEARS

At the very tender age of five; Narmi, though had the faculty but with hazy perception, 'never knew his father'. It was almost like those children stories which his mother used to repeat beneath the full moon nights.

> 'Your father died just after a week of your birth'

> So it was Narmi, who became the 'apple of his mother's eye', among the three children; Neyang the eldest in the family, and Nai the youngest. Narmi, lean and scaly by birth was always given the 'best part of occasional boiled-chicken', and was given to drink a lot of meat and vegetable soup by his mother. May be, she wanted her son to be rich and healthy. Narmi, pre-occupied by his mother's love never missed his late father; though often he felt like knowing...

> 'the significance of a father to a son'

In the early seventies, people in the village never knew, 'what education was all about'. They simply ate, drank and slept and cultivated their piece of land. The only thing that made them worried was the weather; incessant rain and occasional drought. Even at the sight of paddies waving and bending to the tunes of wind would bring them broad smiles to reveal the wrinkles on their faces.

The villagers, both young and old, rejoiced only on the occasion of Solung and Aran festival. Otherwise everything remained the same, monotonous and slow. But interestingly, some of the village folks of Rayang seemingly knew the importance of education and schooling. New residential public schools mushroomed in the neighbouring districts of Assam. Rayang, which lay in the foothill plains, sharing boundary with Assam had often been a worst area, because of boundary disputes. And yet peace had to be restored at time through understanding between the two state governments. It was the village head-man, who took the courage to send out one of his son to 'Don Bosco Residential School', at Jonai. Another prosperous farmer took a sound decision to send away his only son to 'Jubilee Model English Medium School'. So, sending their sons and daughters to distant schools became a fashion among the few rich villagers who were influential. Some other village men had started sending their children to 'Vivekananda Kendra Vidhyalaya', at Oyan, which lay at a distance of about 12 kilometers from the village.

It was then the poor mother felt an urge to send her son Narmi, away from home in order to give him a good education and future. But how? As luck would have it, some well-wishers, seeing the family condition informed the mother of a school called CWC, alias Children Welfare Cente at Pasighat. It was an orphanage run by government those days, where twenty or thirty children were nursed and educated. These children were mostly without a father or a mother who came from different villages.

One evening, the mother returned from the field. She looked weary, after the day-long work. Narmi appeared from a corner, sat beside her and pillowed his head in her arms. After remaining silent for a while, she asked:

'Narmi, would you go to school?', 'I feel like sending you away to Pasighat town like the other children'.

'Mam, how can I stay away from your eyes?', the boy asked quietly.

The mother had no answer to this very question. Neyang, the elder daughter who was busy washing vegetables, had been listening to the mother-son conversation at once interrupted.

'Why can't you study away to Pasighat?'

'It's only yesterday that the head man sent his son Tasong away to Jonai…and you belong to the same age group'

'You will study to become a big officer'

Having said this Neyang smiled, changed her tone and added…

'Narmi, once you are in Pasighat you will also learn to speak Hindi like the other town boys'

Narmi innocently giggled and the mother participated in order to encourage the son. After few days the mother decided to go and speak to the school authorities. When the day came, Narmi felt heavy within but at the same time he felt elated and smiled to himself having thought of himself at the scope of seeing Pasighat town; of learning Hindi; and even of the electricity. Narmi was also happy for one thing, it would be his first ever longest journey. Travelling 37 kilometers from Ruksin check-post to Pasighat by bus would be a thrilling journey to him. Narmi, with great excitement occupied the window seat just behind the driver. The mother sat in the middle and Neyang in the left corner. Looking out from the speedy bus Narmi cried pointing.

'Mam, see.., see…', 'The trees are running backward!'

'Don't look towards the ground, you will feel giddy and vomit', the mother warned the son.

Within two hours the bus reached Pasighat. Narmi's happiness knew no bound after setting his foot for the first time in that strange land. The beautiful Pasighat, yet in its growing stage of urbanization fascinated Narmi the most. The well-planned market area, shops and stalls, the sweet meat sellers, the statue of Mahatma Gandhi in the heart of the bazaar, different faces and cuts, the shrill cries of the Anchal Samity buses, Mahindra jeeps, Ambassador cars and Premier Padmini. The lined-up government quarters and office buildings that looked different from the stilted thatched roofed huts that Narmi had seen in his own village. Narmi got himself lost in his own thoughts so much so that he paid a deaf ear to the mother-daughter conversation. But Narmi at once called out as if awaken from a long slumber.

'Aye! Mam, who is that bald man made of stone?'

'That's the man whom do we sing, '*goo rooja pabona, Gandhi rooja pabona*!' the mother replied instantly.

'He is the man who gave us the freedom', she added.

The son pondered at the mention of words like…'*Gandhi and freedom'*. He had no idea what the mother was telling. So, he changed the topic as they walked along the black topped road. It was then the mother decided to have something as they were already hungry. Narmi's mouth had already began watering even before entering a canteen where they had sweet Rasgollas, the mother's favourite.

Beneath the clear blue sky, Pasighat appeared more beautiful than ever; the flowering trees giving cool shade to tired pedestrians along the road, and even more charming were the sweet fragrances of flowers brought into the nostrils of Narmi by the cool breezes of the mighty Siang river. Narmi's heart was full that day. He was living in the present, feeling it and experiencing it. It was a wonderful day, a memory to be cherished even in the later part of his life.

They got the school at around 10.30 a.m. The school authorities of the C.W.C. accepted Narmi without much formalities and he was given a seat in the hostel. Miss Yanung, the hostel warden was asked to take care of the new comer. By 3 p.m. the daughter and the mother had to part from Narmi as they had to catch the last bus for Ruksin. Narmi, having learnt that the mother was departing, took a heavy sigh and sobbed bitterly. Though felt heavy within, the mother and daughter tried to console Narmi but in vain. So, she silently pushed a ten rupee note into Narmi's pocket. Neyang, the elder sister didn't say anything. Though her eyes were filled, she finally gathered some strength and said:

'We will visit you at the end of every month', and they hurried towards the public bus stand.

CHAPTER TWO

AT CWC PASIGHAT

Yanung the hostel warden, was a spinster in her thirties. She had a heart of gold and cared all the children like her own child. She was helping the boy to get adjusted to the new environment. Narmi was allotted Bed No.3 at the hostel. Though less spoken, he soon soothed himself to the new world. He made new friends and mingled with Otin, Tojing, Nanung and Oyon. His 'home-sickness 'did not last long and he started enjoying the hostel life. Thus he was gripped in the world of innocence and ignorance. His mother was everything that he needed in the life. Love, care and comfort and even the demand for small small things were fulfilled by the mother. She was like an angel guarding him all the way.

Everyone has a tale to tell, so had Narmi. Misfortunes and agonies have always been a part of Narmi's life but there are some funny episodes in his life which would make us sympathise and laugh. The first night at the CWC hostel was one of the bitterest moment of his life, most scary and yet memorable. Narmi, after supper went to his bed. Sleeping on a cot was something new to him. He couldn't sleep that night and had to roll from one edge of the cot to another. Whenever he closed his eyes he saw the picture of his mother, sister and younger brother Nai. He saw endless dreams; sometimes he saw his mother waving him goodbye and disappearing in the far horizon and sometimes he saw himself playing with Nai. And at one moment he saw that he was walking in a vast desert all alone, tired, hungry and thirsty. He was tracking a path that led him to nowhere. On the way he felt very much to piss, and was searching for a proper spot to release his urine. At that very moment he woke up and snapped himself from the dream. He found himself on the bed, kicked off his quilt somewhere and he knew that he was awake. He looked around but it was pitch dark everywhere. Narmi tried to penetrate his eye through the dark but he couldn't. He was deadly feeling urination and his urinary bladder grew bigger and bigger giving him unbearable pressure. He wanted to release, to be at ease at the earliest. But how? He was new to the hostel, to the environment. He had no idea about the edges and turns of the hostel, he got confused about the position of the door and the windows. Narmi was completely blinded. Hunching, he tried to search the switch board, moved his fingers around. Sometimes he would move his fingers feeling along the walls; the walls that seemed never ending. He fainted to release. It was really hard for him to carry. He knew he would be punished if he did so but it was not only the fear of the punishment. His inner voice wouldn't allow him for such a shameful act. He crawled around the hostel hall, passed through boys that lay like corpses, wrapped in quilts. He searched for the door, the switch board to put the light on but failed. Even the tick of a second in the wall clock seemed hour to him. His tummy wouldn't bear it anymore, so ultimately he had to release his urine somewhere in a corner.

'Oh, my god!', said Narmi after spreading his piss beneath someone's bed and he crawled back to his own bed. That was a nightmare, a bitter experience that haunted him for a long time. He had thrown away the big burden that was troubling him for the last 15 minutes and now he was free. But Narmi didn't know where he had exactly released. The following morning he got up quite early and stealthily noticed that there was a little stagnant pool beneath Tason's cot.

'wow! what's this?', said Tason. 'It didn't rain last night'.

'I don't see any cracks up there!', said Otin looking at the ceiling.

'It stinks', said Tojing staring the pool with examining eyes.

'Urine, urine oh, it's urine', cried Otin giving Tason a doubtful look.

Tason gave back a frown, almost angry; while Narmi who knew the secret was trying to avoid the whole discussion by keeping himself busy with morning ablutions. He walked to and fro as if in a Hindi cinema waiting for someone, cutting himself off from the scene! The story doesn't end here, there are many such instances of his hostel life that would make him a laugh-at stuff, but for him bitter and ugly. On one occasion the hostel superintendent, after spotting a sugar particle on Narmi's chin asked.

'Narmi, did you take sugar?'

'No, I didn't', replied Narmi.

'Are you sure?', asked Tazep again in a louder voice.

'Yes'

'Promise, you are not lying', warned Tazep.

'Yes, I do', said Narmi in a shaky voice.

Narmi was trembling inside, but he was pretending to be bold enough to come up with answers for every queries. He tried to gather all his might to stop his two skinny legs from shaking. Tazep then disappeared for a second and called Tojing.

'Tojing, where you?'

'Coming sir….'

'Bring that looking mirror hanged on the wall'

'Yes sir', said Tojing.

Neither Narmi nor Tojing knew what the hostel superintendent was going to do with the mirror. They were simply confused and stood dumb and still because Tazep was on many occasion; a strict, less spoken and harsh person. Then after a while, looking stern he went straight to Narmi and asked indicating two or three sugar particle stucking on the chin.

'What is this?', asked Tazep pointing to the shiny particles.

'Look into the mirror!', 'Don't you see something unusual on your face?'

Narmi now knew why Tazep had brought the mirror infront of his face. His nerve got loose and started shaking like anything. His face turned red because of fear mixed with embarrassment. He knew he would be beaten or whipped for stealing sugar from the kitchen. Narmi almost cried and the other boys stood still without even moving their eye balls. Every one expected a punishment for Narmi but to their surprise Tazep padded Narmi and simply said:

'Next time don't dare to repeat the same'.

Tazep himself in order to comfort the boy started laughing and the boys followed him in surprise. Thus Tazep was a real nut, crude outside but soft inside. He would easily sympathise a boy and at times encourage the children to study hard for their better future. Not only that, he would always stand by them whenever they needed his support. He was a godfather to many of the poor boys at CWC.

Narmi hated medicine. He would simply vomit at the sight of a white round tablet or coloured capsules while holding them in his hand. Tazep was the only person who could handle this. He would have the crushed medicine in one of his palm, another boy would be standing near with a glass of water, and yet another boy with a spoon of sugar. First Narmi was led to drink some water, then Tazep after asking Narmi to keep his mouth wide open; would throw the powdered medicine inside, then keeping no time gap, another boy would throw in the sugar. This was the only technique to make Narmi have the medicine whenever he got sick. To him it was a physical trauma, a punishment more than being sick in bed. Thus hostel life at Pasighat for Narmi was full of lively experiences. Sometimes he would laugh and sometimes he would cry. Watching Hindi movies became a routine work, so much so that books and studies became a thing secondary to him.

CHAPTER THREE

THE TURNING POINT

One morning, on 25th December Narmi had a surprise call from the Hostel warden.

'Narmi, where are you?', 'Your uncle has come from the village to see you'

Narmi came running from a corner and said,' Oh! Iam here!'

'What's the matter?', Narmi asked with curious innocence.

Narmi was quite happy and excited to see his uncle at the visitor's room unaware of the news that he was going to hear. He thought his mother had sent him something from the village.

'Aye! uncle, you're here at this hour to see me?', asked Narmi smiling.

Tamat hesitated to open his mouth but he had to do it against his will. He knew, they had to hurry back.

'Narmi, I came here to take you home', he said in a shaky voice.

'Your mother has passed away this morning', 'She died at the Ruksin hospital'.

Narmi got stunned to hear this. He couldn't utter even a single word and stood still like a statue. The news was too much for a little boy like him to bear. He shook his head and almost collapsed. It was Tamat, the uncle who caught him in his arms. Holding him tight he tried to console the boy, but in vain. Narmi felt a hollow depression running down his ribs and felt the whole aura turning black. He didn't say a word and got ready to follow his uncle. Yanung the hostel warden tried to comfort the boy but her soft words didn't work this time.

Tamat took permission from the hostel superintendent and walked back to the Public bus stand. They found an empty Shaktiman truck heading towards Ruksin. They boarded the truck but stood gravely without exchanging a single word, and the truck rolled on. Many countless thoughts came up in Narmi's mind but he couldn't make out what they exactly were. They were all empty, hollow thoughts without a beginning or an end. The only thing he could make out was that; from now on he would be alone and there would be no one to wipe his tears whenever he cries. Thinking all these things he only felt like crying and nothing else.

Soon the truck reached Ruksin and they had to cycle again covering a distance of about half a kilometer. Finally they reached the spot. At a distance Narmi could see so many people gathered and still gathering in the Christian graveyard. Narmi's heart started throbbing like anything. He could hear the cries of men, women and children who were his close relatives. Still nearer he could hear people praying to Christ to give the departed soul peace and eternal life followed by the chorus:

"Donyi e…….. nyokyimang

Neyang e…….yayimang,

Mingke suna kidie jisume karikkue;

Kamporuna un dolung delo"

Coming closer, Narmi had a look at the coffin with white shroud spread already brought down to be cremated. He couldn't control himself, cried louder and staggered. He saw Neyang and

Nai crying under someone's arm in helpless situation. Narmi knew that they would be alone in this world with no one to stand beside them and lean upon. He could hear the Christian brothers passing different comments who were witnessing the whole scene at close range.

'Oh god, have mercy on these children!'

'Who will shoulder the responsibility of raising these orphans?'

'Don't know', 'Only god knows!'

'Perhaps their uncle would do!', 'but where are they?', asked someone.

'I don't see any uncle around here!'

'Yes of course', said the other.

'How did she die?', '… of malaria?'

'May be'

'But people say she was ill only for three or four days'

'No, she died because of evil spirit', someone commented.

'Perhaps Neyang will be the mother to her two brothers', said one with a grin.

'Bullshit, she too is very young!'

The villagers uttered all kinds of sympathetic words but nobody had the actual courage to take any responsibility. Of course they had their own burdens and more over most of them were poor cultivators. Soon after the rites, the Christian brothers and sisters disappeared one by one. Nobody dared to come near to these children and comfort them as they feared responsibility would fall on them. The same evening, people came and prayed for peace for the passed soul and for the family. As it is customary, they brought with them biscuits, tea and sugar for the evening fellowship. It went for some three or four days. Some people tried to console and gave advice and yet others stared the children with silence and sympathy. But soon the villagers stopped visiting these children and turned themselves to their routine activities of livelihood. Their sympathy died and no one bothered to enquire about them. They were alone. No uncle, no aunt, no nephew, no niece and no close relatives and friends. Neyang, who was not even 19 became a mother to her two little brothers. The call of the hour made her grow old each day and so she got matured ahead of her time. She had to quit her studies to earn her daily bread. Though she was good in studies and a favorite student to many of the teachers, she had to sacrifice a dream she had never hunted. Like a mother, she only wanted to see her little brothers' smile and keep their belly full so that they do not steal or do anything against the society. So, Neyang ultimately had to step out of the village looking out for greener pastures to support herself and her two little brothers.

CHAPTER FOUR
NEW DESTINATION

'Narmi, you must go back to your school', said Neyang one evening.

'I don't know what would I do', replied Narmi.

'Be brave!', 'What has happened has happened'.

'May be it was god's will!'.

'You see, I'am always there for you', Neyang added.

'But why is god so unmerciful to us?', Narmi gasped.

Nai, the youngest was listening to all these conversations like a dump lamb. He was not even seven to understand all those changes in the house. He only felt a kind of desperation at nightfall and felt his mother would return one day or the other. It is at this time that Narmi reveals Neyang about BKMS; a bigger orphanage where they had to be admitted.

Boum Kakir Mission was a residential school meant for the orphans. There were more than two hundred students like Narmi, who came from different quarters. It was a real training ground for many of the hopeless girls and boys whose parents were no more. Many qualified teachers from all over were engaged in helping these children in building character, discipline, self esteem and above all making them recognizing the value of hard work.

'People say BKMS is 75 kilometers away from Pasighat', said Narmi.

'Yes, it's in *Adi Among*', added Neyang who had some rough idea about the place.

'Study hard, very hard', 'Through studies only, you can be counted as a human being in our society', Neyang advised the brother like a mother.

Narmi listened to all these silently and was trying to lock each word permanently in his mind. Every little word was precious and Narmi treasured them where ever he went. One morning as Narmi was getting ready to leave for Pasighat; Nai, the younger brother though innocent sensed his going away from home and started weeping.

'Nai, Narmi will be back soon!'

'He will bring you lot of sweets and new clothes when he return', Neyang said while trying to reconcile the child. Nai calmed down at the mention of sweets and new clothes as these things were out of their reach and they could have them only in their dreams.

Soon Narmi returned to CWC Pasighat. Yanung the Hostel warden gave Narmi a warm welcome on his return and paid more attention this time, in order to divert the boy's mind from sad thoughts and feelings of emptiness. The death of the mother had a great impact on the boy. Narmi wasn't that casual and carefree boy now, he rather became ambitious. He gave up watching Amitabh, Mithun, and Rajnikanth movies at Latbong Cinema Hall. He was into studies though he was a mediocre student.

As days rolled by, the authorities of CWC decided to take the students to BKMS Boleng. The boys were excited and curious about the school and the place. But none had the idea, only Narmi could form some rough idea about the place…'*Adi Among*', or the '*Land of the Adis*'. One evening the boys sat together and started discussing about the new school they were to be admitted. The boys were inquisitive and started putting endless queries to Narmi who was the supposed leader of the group.

'Where is *Adi Among*?', asked Otin who was quite dull in comparison to others.

'There!', said Narmi pointing towards the window.

'Ha! Ha! Ha!'

The boys then burst into a loud guffaw staring at Otin who became angry feeling insulted.

'How's the place?', asked Mongol.

'It's a real beauty. Mountains everywhere, streams and rivers!', explained Narmi with confidence.

'Woh! We could go fishing every day', added Tojing.

'Rivers are dangerous there, you cannot go near them', advised Narmi.

'We will have the chance to see *Eso*', added Otin with a glow on his face.

'I heard the roads are very narrow and winding', said Tojing.

'Yes, it's dangerous and risky'.

'If a bus misses the track it goes down!', added Narmi.

'Where?', asked Otin curiously.

'To Siang river!', answered Narmi and added.

'The hills and plantain leaves are said to be the abode of evil spirits!'.

The boys came closer to each other at the mention of evil spirits; as Nanung, a senior girl student had come under the influence of evil spirits one month ago.

'Oh! I forgot to tell you about the Armies in *Adi Among*', said Narmi with fear and excitement.

'Do you know they chase young girls if they spot them?'.

'They would tie rags around their penis before raping them', added Narmi.

'I too heard that from my elder brother', said Mongol.

'In *Adi Among* young girls hide and throw away their baskets of firewood at the sight of approaching Army trucks', told Narmi.

'Do they don't have mothers or sisters?', added Tani agitated.

While these boys were immersed in conversation, switching from one topic to another, Otin who was nodding for a long time bade good night to his friends and went to bed. Then one by one the boys disappeared from the spot like the birds do at sunset looking for the night shelter.

⊷⊰◈⊱⊶

After a month, a day was fixed and the children of CWC Pasighat were taken to BKMS Boleng which lay at a distance of about 75 km from Pasighat. Narmi, Otin, Nanung, Tojing, Tasam, Oyon and Mongol were all excited about the new school and the place. Tazep the Hostel superintendent was to escort the boys to Boleng which numbered around fifteen, all orphans.

'Children, your tickets have been booked', called Tazep on the day fixed.

'Put all your belongings inside your trunks and see you don't miss anything', he added.

'At what time are we moving sir?', asked Tasam who was eldest among the students.

'At eight, by State Transport', replied Tazep.

'The bus comes here to pick you up as they don't have other passengers', said Tazep.

While the boys were busy packing their belongings, Yanung the Hostel warden was watching the whole scene silently from a corner. She was solemn and her eyes were filled looking at the boys. She wondered what the future has in store for these children; and that she would never see these boys again. The cook who used to cook for these boys was there too, watching the boys packing their belongings. Then Tazep appeared somewhere from a corner and said.

'Boys, the bus comes here. We have to move'.

'Have you packed your belongings Narmi?', asked Yanung in her usual soft voice.

'Yes miss', replied Narmi.

Tazep then clapped his hand to draw the boys' attention and said.

'Boys your miss has her last word, so pay attention'.

Moving forward with a heavy heart Yanung shared her last words of advice to the boys. She was always soft spoken and the boys liked her very much and as for Narmi she was like a real mother.

'My dear children, may be this would be our last meeting. So, always remember my word. Believe in yourself and in god. Be good, be sincere, and hard working. One day you will have time to smile to yourself. Respect your elders and especially your teachers and get their good wishes and blessings. And one last word, if you visit Pasighat don't forget to visit me'. With these words she stepped back aside and finally said in a low tone.

'Good bye children. Have a good journey!'.

Having spoken these words she became touched and emotional and started weeping. Narmi and the other boys ran to her, clasped her and started crying loudly. Tazep, standing still watched the whole drama silently and said.

'Boys come!'.

The boys waved good bye to Yanung and picked up their belongings and headed for the bus parked at Solung ground. The bus conductor and the cook helped the boys in putting their trunks into the bus. Otin and Narmi rushed, pulling and pushing at each other to occupy the seat just behind the driver, Narmi's fovourite seat.

'I will sit near the window', begged Otin looking at Narmi.

'It's okay. But if I vomit let me be here', urged Narmi.

'Why not!', said Otin with approval.

Thus the boys forgot Miss Yanung and her tears for a moment at the prospect of seeing their new school and the new place. They were excited and happy. Yanung watching their childish nature and innocence was happy too. She bade them good bye and called out loudly.

'Happy journey boys!'

'Thank you, miss!', the boys said in unison.

The conductor blew his whistle and the bus rolled forward. Yanung, the cook and the others stared at the bus till it got disappeared. The bus sped towards GTC but stopped at Dangaria Baba Temple. Travelers heading for *Adi Among*, either on foot or vehicle usually stop and pray here for their safety. It was believed that a big black cobra housed the huge tree where the temple located. The driver stopped the bus in front of the temple and went inside with some incense sticks and later came out with a big red tikka smeared on his forehead; and in his hand were some Prasad from the pujari. Some women went inside and did the same. Narmi and the other boys looked around the temple with Tazep. Then, after sometime the driver sat behind the wheel and the bus giving a loud hiss rolled towards the *Land of the Adis*. It was a lethargic ride, the route being narrow and altitude becoming higher and higher. The boys began chattering picking up many different topics.

'Why did the bus stop there?', asked Narmi.

Otin, who belonged to a neighboring village of Pasighat seemed confident in answering the question. He began explaining...

'Long time ago, some travelers were stopped by an wild elephant in the middle of the road near Rengging village....'.

'Why?', asked Narmi being curious.

'They didn't stop and pray at Dangaria Baba temple', replied Otin.

Then Otin went on saying that people of all castes come and pray in this temple. Even marital ceremonies were performed and interestingly new vehicles even before their registration are brought here for poojas, in order to avoid untoward incidents.

The bus giving a loud deafening roar was climbing rather slowly. The driver spreading his huge arms, sitting behind the wheel was trying hard to negotiate the sharp turns and the narrow route. He was a tall man, well built and with a heavy moustache. The journey for the boys was not that exciting as they thought. So they enjoyed the scenic beauty outside the bus window. Whenever they looked out of the window their eyes were blocked by big hills and green mountains. The tall trees, streams, valleys and rows of green and blue hills enchanted Narmi the most. On the right side, below, some few hundred meters down, the mighty Siang River appeared like a silver snake following them throughout the journey.

'Oh, look there! an *Eso*!', cried Otin pointing to the look alike Yak, a semi domesticated animal.

'Wow, it's beautiful', chorused the boys looking out.

'Oh, there's another there!', cried out Mongol as if he had discovered something new.

Thus the boys were trying to spot something or the other peeping out of the window to feel a sense of superiority amongst them and be elated later. Except for Nanung, who sat silently in a corner didn't participate. The boys were enjoying spotting *Eso*, which is a yard stick to measure the rich among the locales. And they were excited because these semi domesticated large animal are not found in the plains.

The bus after a long exhausted crawl, with hisses and loud roars reached *Nogyin Erak,* a dangerous sinking and sliding zone which falls on the way to Rengging village. This zone has always been popular among the hill tribes, not for its scenic beauty but for taking the lives of many. This round the clock moist and muddy, sliding zone has been a fear among the passers for many years. You lose track and you lose your life. Boulders, pebbles, and mud would roll down at any moment without a warning and would bring an end a trespasser. With death lurking around, and river Siang awaiting down below with her cruel smile was a nightmare scenario.

Finally the driver and the passengers had a sigh of relief after crossing the danger zone.

'Wah! Hum bach gaya', the driver said elated.

'I didn't look down even!', said Tojing.

'I with my eyes closed was praying to god', said Nanung turning to the boys with a smile.

'Death would come to all of us one day', said Tazep to the boys.

'But it should not come early!', replied Otin with a sense of humour which made the others' laugh.

After the horrifying *Nogyin Erak*, the bus somehow rolled on rather slowly. The driver maneuvered every turns and curls with great attention. The boys then started chatting again picking up many different topics. Nanung was already asleep, her head nodding and sometimes hitting against the edge of the bus. Later the boys had an overdose of greeneries around them. The frequent climbing up and climbing down, the twist and turns made the boys giddy. Narmi had already a spread of vomitting on the floor of the bus which gave an extra duty to the handyman. But such were common phenomena that a traveler had to face in this part of the world. Thus after hours of languorous ride and struggle the bus reached Boleng at around 1.30 p.m. The driver dropped Tazep and his boys at Boleng Inspection Bunglow as there was no other passenger.

'Boys this is Boleng and it's a beautiful place', said Tazep turning to the boys.

The boys including lone girl Nanung were happy seeing the new place and environment but Narmi grew quite emotional and one could easily read looking at his face. Boleng had an EAC Post and was still in the growing stage of urbanization. There were few government buildings and establishments which scattered here and there in an unorganized manner. The little town laid on a slanting hill and in the edge down below one could still see Siang flowing south.

'Where is our Pasighat?', asked Tasam laughing.

'Yes, really', added Tojing hoping Tazep would come up with an answer.

'It's there', said Tazep pointing to the direction where Siang flowed.

'Boys have a wash. We're going to have our lunch', he said after sometime.

'Oh! my god, am terribly hungry', said Otin touching his pot bellied stomach.

'Me too', followed Nanung.

There was a large dining table inside which accommodated all and the boys were happy being together. The smell of fish curry in the air had already doubled the boys' hunger even before the food arrived on the table. Otin's mouth began watering which he tried to hide with a cough and had a glass of water. The boys sensing, giggled at his habit.

'Khana aa gaya', the cook said in jolly mood.

'Aur chahiye to bhi boolna, ha?', he added.

So the boys had their belly full. Otin didn't leave a single rice on the plate.

'Boys, now take some rest', said Tazep after the lunch, and added.

'Your teachers from BKMS would come in the evening to see you'.

'Be presentable and disciplined', he warned the boys and went to his room.

The boys too went to the room allotted to them except for Nanung who was given a private room being a girl. The boys after some loud chattering went into a deep sleep feeling exhausted. Their afternoon nap was disturbed by a knock on the door after three and half hour by Tazep.

'Boys, get up now and get yourself made up', said Tazep with a knock on the door.

'Get up-get up, boys!', said Tasam waking up his friends.

'What's up now?', said Mongol feeling irritated and rubbing his eyes.

'Teachers are coming to see us!', replied Tasam.

The boys got up. Narmi half asleep felt that he was still in Pasighat. Otin yet on bed was busy breaking his joints, waist and neck that gave a thud sound and which showed his laziness. But soon he joined the boys after wash. Then Tazep gathered the boys and gave a few words of advice to the students.

'Boys, teachers from BKMS are arriving to see and talk to you'.

'Don't feel shy. Answer every queries they put', he dictated.

Then he started guiding the boys from one thing to another. He spoke on discipline, manners, self respect and importance of hard work in life. He also reminded the boys to remember his word as it would be their last moment of being together.

At sharp 6 pm in the evening three teachers from BKMS arrived to see the boys. They first met Tazep who was their escort and had some private conversation inside. Then they entered the boys' room.

'Boys, your teachers have come', Tazep informed waving and indicating.

'Good evening, sir', the boys said in chorus.

'Good evening boys', the teachers responded with a smile.

Then Mr. Pradhan came forward and started asking the names of the boys one by one. Then they turned to Nanung, the lone girl in the group of eight boys.

'What's your name?', asked Mr. Pradhan.

'My..my.. name Nanung', answered Nanung in broken English blushing and looking aside.

The boys giggled which made Nanung uncomfortable. Then Mr. Singh came up and supported Nanung.

'Smart girl, you speak good English!', said Mr. Singh.

'What did you say your name?', asked Mr. Mitra turning to Narmi.

'Narmi, Sir!', replied Narmi.

'Good name. What does it stand for?', asked Mr. Mitra.

'Ah… Boy! Sir', answered Narmi.

'Good'

'What is your hobby?', asked Mitra.

'I like drawing sir!'.

'Very good!'.

'Yours', asked Mitra blinking to Otin.

'I like football', Otin replied.

Then Mitra and Pradhan started putting different questions to each boy ranging from their hobbies to their favourite subject. Mr. Mitra was soft spoken. He was a true gentleman, which one could make out easily. Mr. Pradhan was outspoken and humorous sort and Mr. Singh, very supportive and patronizing.

'So, boys we see you in the school tomorrow', said Mr. Pradhan while leaving.

'Good night teachers!', said the boys in unison.

'Yes, good night'.

There was an air of silence in the atmosphere after the teachers had left. The boys had their supper and went to bed at eight. Narmi had a hard night. The new school, new place and atmosphere were something that he couldn't swallow down easily. He missed his little brother Nai and Neyang, who was more than a sister. Yet night being made for rest and sleep, Narmi finally had to.

Next morning the boys got up early, had their ablutions and under the guidance of escort Tazep headed for BKMS. They were received by Mr. Pradhan at the Principal's office. After some paper works and official formalities the boys were admitted to the school. Nanung was left under the charge of Miss Roy, who was the hostel warden. Then boys were supplied with basic necessities like bedding, quilt, blanket and even pillows. Mr. Pradhan, who was the boys' warden allocated hostel seats to the boys. He also introduced the new comers to other students and went away after telling them to get ready for the school.

Narmi was allotted a seat in Block No.2. There were about 30 boys in that block. He was very fortunate to meet Talen and Talung, who hailed from the same village. He also met new friends like Karik, Karge, Joluk and Rijum who were his classmates. They were all helpful in getting him adjusted to the new place. The school began at 8 am with a morning prayer. Then newspaper reading by a senior student, followed by morning thought delivered by Meena Koje with the lines, 'Hard work is the only key to success in life', simply sitting on the ground and thinking of catching the stars will not help, we will have to come out and work..'. These lines had a permanent impression on Narmi which stayed with him throughout life. After the morning thought Mr. Rao the principal, spoke like a military adviser, which were equally inspiring. Then finally the national anthem echoed in the air which could be heard even from a good distance. Narmi had his introduction to 3rd standard and he had a great day at the new school. Though nothing remarkable happened, he was satisfied with his friends and teachers.

Narmi was allotted the cot next to Taking who hailed from Rengging village. 'Hi, I'm Taking from Rengging village', introduced Taking extending his hand. 'I'm in standard four', he added.

'I'm Narmi. I'm from Rayang', Narmi replied with a smile.

'Do you know Talen and Talung? 'asked Taking.

'Yes of course, they are from Rayang', Narmi answered becoming more ease.

Narmi was quiet most of the time and by nature a bit reserved and so it was Taking who did most of the talking. Taking was out spoken and talkative and this broke even Narmi's silence and thus they became good friends in the school. Narmi met yet another new comer Takeng, a tall boy who was quite senior to him in age, wearing a short pant and a wrist watch in his hand. Takeng who came from nearby Dosing village was like an elder brother to Narmi. So by now Narmi had a bunch of good friends around and at least for sometime he forgot that he was an orphan. The routine work of rising up early, doing PT, morning study hour, library period and music class and recreation and sports hour were all designed to give the best shape to a child. The whole system and administration of the school was perfect, and destined to give a perfect mould to child and those who failed to be a part of this system was very unfortunate.

CHAPTER FIVE

INSIGHT STORIES

As it's said, *'Every coin has two sides'*, Narmi was shocked to discover the other. Every block had a Prefect and they were christened CAPTAINS and Tani was the Captain of Block No.2 where Narmi had his cot. One afternoon as Narmi was heading for school after the lunch he had a surprise call.

'Narmi, Captain is calling you', Tati said rushing to him.

'Be quick, run back to the hostel', he added gasping.

Narmi being new and obedient, without any queries rushed back to the hostel. Seeing Tani, who was a big bruiser and the Captain he politely asked.

'Captain did you call me?', Narmi asked.

As soon as Tani saw Narmi, he clenched his fist and without a word and warning gave a big blow on Narmi's forehead. Within a second it formed into a big red bump, and seeing it one could measure how it must have pained Narmi. Narmi started crying loudly but he never knew the reasons behind. He kept thinking why he was beaten. He felt helpless and orphaned again. He thought of retaliating but he was too small for that.

'Go back to school! don't cry!', Tani yelled with a warning.

'If you let the teachers' know, you get harder hit later', Tani warned again.

Narmi had no choice. He had to wipe his tears and returned to the afternoon class. He tried to hide the big red bump feeling shy but couldn't. The boys knowing the reason tried not to notice the bump on Narmi's head and were silent but the girl student kept staring at Narmi. It made Narmi nervous and dejected.

'Narmi, what's up? You have a big bump on your forehead!', asked Mr. Pradhan the geography teacher.

The boys stared at each other fearing Narmi would reveal the long preserved secret. But to their relief came out with the reply.

'I rushed in a hurry and hit the side walls', Narmi said in a low tone looking sideways.

'O.K. next time you be very careful Narmi', Mr. Pradhan said with a smile.

'Hurry doesn't solve worry', Mr. Pradhan added, which brought laughter to the whole class.

The same day, at around four in the evening, Narmi overheard some boys discussing the burning topic of the day. He now came to know the reason why he was beaten by the Captain. The routine work was not followed. Some boys forgot to clean the Captain's plate after lunch. Narmi was confused to discover that a single mistake done by a single boy could bring so much pain to so many boys of the hostel. Narmi now became a part of this routine work. Like the tongs of a machine he now performed his duties perfectly at regular intervals of time. Whether, of keeping the plates ready, cleaning the plate after meal or breakfast, placing the bottle of boiled water at the specific corner where the Captain sat, and of late night massage. More than school homework, these were the tasks that boys did without any complain. Yes, Narmi became more aware and well informed of all in order to avoid yet another pinching blow from the Captain.

One day it was Taking and Narmi's turn. Taking being a senior at the school and more experienced was acting like an adviser and a teacher. As Narmi was about to sweep Captain Tani's room, Taking stopped him halfway and said as if he was the master.

'Narmi, you need not sweep the Captains' room'.

'I'll sweep his room', Taking said almost pulling Narmi.

'Why?', asked Narmi with a surprise look.

'I don't want to see a big bump on your forehead again', replied Taking with a giggle.

Then turning again to Narmi, he said in a serious tone.

'You know, I'm here for the last one year. I know how things work'.

'Narmi, you simply pile up the books and keep them in proper place', advised Taking seeing the Captain's table scattered with books, pens and geometry box'.

After the broom session, Narmi and Taking went to the dining hall to place the Captain's ultra cleaned plate at the Captain's specific seat, placed a bottle of clean drinking water as it was time for the evening meal. As usual, the meal was served at around seven. Boys would rush to the dining hall at the stroke of the bell, say their prayers quickly and would swallow up any item provided to them. Yes, why would a hungry stomach look for taste and color? Teachers like Mr. Pradhan, Mitra, Nathan, Singh and Roy made their timely rounds but what went behind the curtains were beyond the understanding of these teachers too. With the teachers gone, the Captain also got up from the table after having his meal finished. Narmi obediently picked up the Captain's plate and Taking collected the water bottle and the glass tumbler. There were crowd of boys at the water tap outside cleaning their plates and tumbler. Taking, like an army made his way straight through the crowd pushing his plates forward and said warningly.

'Side, side, side please… the Captain's plate'.

Then he let Narmi to wash the Captain's plate and a little later cleaned their own. It was something magical that Narmi experienced in his whole life. At the mention of the word *Captain*, the boys subsided making way for Narmi and Taking. Narmi, who was a new comer, was like an apprentice to Taking. Every day he was learning something new at the school, about the school, at the hostel and about the seniors. Thus Narmi discovered that the Captains led a king size life at the orphanage though ironically they themselves were real orphans. Whether the authorities and the teachers knew or not was not an important question. Hooliganism and dictatorship existed among the Captains like Tani of Block No.2, Taki of No.1 and Takut of No.3. The whole system was operated with great secrecy and every new comers and juniors were its victim. Bullying a junior for nothing was a very common event at the school. Narmi many a times felt humiliated as he never washed others' plate in his life prior to BKMS. He had his sister Neyang who did most of the washing job at home.

The same thing happened at Block No.1 after two days. At 7.30 p.m. all the boys were asked to stand in line by Captain Taki, and Tasong was helping the Captain in conveying his message.

'Whose turn was today?', Taki asked in a loud harsh voice.

The boys were silent. Nobody dared to answer. There was a pin drop silence. Otin could hear his heart thumping and his legs started shaking vigorously though he knew he was not to be blame for.

'Whose turn was today?', the Captain repeated walking to and fro like Gabbar Singh of *Sholay* with a cane in his hand.

The boys knowing the prey looked at each other and were making their gesture towards Taling to avoid being beaten. Finally Taling stepped forward and confessed that it was Tasup and his turn but they forgot the routine. Taling was shaking and trembling and bending low he begged excuse in his little husky voice.

'Captain, I'm sorry! It was our turn. We forgot the routine'.

'Who's your partner?', Captain asked in a loud shaky voice out of rage.

'Tasup', answered Taling.

The boys looked around gazing at each other but Tasup was nowhere to be seen. The next moment one could hear was the sound of whipping and helpless cry of pain that came from Taling. Taling was beaten from top to bottom in front of everyone.

'Aya! Ooh! Aah!', cried Taling but nobody came to his rescue.

'I promise, promise... Captain. I'll not repeat', begged Taling kneeling down and pulling his ears apart like a rubber.

The boys watched the whole drama without a word. Otin out of fear passed a few drop of urine to wet his pant and thus became a center of mockery throughout his days at BKMS. Then the Captain warned again.

'Boys! This is just a trailer. You will enjoy the full episode next time'.

The Captain then made a gesture and all the boys disappeared one by one. Taling left alone, crawled to his bed sobbing bitterly. Late at night, at around 10 p.m. Tasup crept back stealthily to his bed. He knew what would be the result. So he was hiding somewhere in a dark corner. But he had his share in the morning and didn't escape from the Captain's whip. Seeing him beaten Taking whispered to Narmi.

'Kanoon ka hath lamba hota hain', and they burst into a silent laughter.

But if one overlook this terror of self styled dictatorship and hooliganism from the selected seniors, BKMS was a paradise for many of the orphans like Narmi, Otin or Taking. BKMS was an umbrella, where different tribes from Arunachal Pradesh sheltered together. There were no distinctions between the so called Adi, Pasi, Padam, Galo, Nyishi, Tagin or Hillmiri. It was an open space where the orphans outlet their hidden energy and talents. It was a furnance where boys could be given any desired shape. By now Narmi had become quite ambitious and put more of his energy into studies. Though very young, he understood his position. Being alone and deprived of parental love and care, he knew what he wanted in his life. BKMS gave him the opportunity, the freedom of thought and the space to outlet his hidden urges. Thus he got matured ahead of his time and age. Most of the time Narmi's mind was occupied and he seldom found time for evil and unconstructive thoughts. He was an excellent artist and through various paintings he sometimes expressed his thoughts and emotions.

One Sunday morning as Narmi was alone in the hostel busy painting a scenery, he heard Tamar calling and looking out for Karik.

'Karik, where are you?', Tamar said making his round.

'Karik, where are you? Your mother has come to see you', Tamar said again in a loud voice.

The hostel was all empty. Some boys were watching television, some washing their clothes and yet others busy playing. Narmi was just about to give a finishing touch to a scenery when he heard Karik coming in with his mother and younger sister Karie. Narmi though busy overheard the conversation that went between the mother, son and the daughter. He came to know that they had come a long way from Darka village, West Siang to visit Karik. After a few minutes of the happy family reunion, Karik called out.

'Narmi, please come and join us'.

Narmi being timid, hesitated but couldn't decline the invitation. He got up and joined Karik.

'This is my mother and younger sister Karie', Karik introduced to his friend.

'They have come to see me from Darka', he added smiling.

Narmi smiled back to them shyly without a word.

'Son, where are you from?', Karik's mother asked.

'I'm from Rayang', Narmi replied with a smile.

'We are classmates', Narmi added having nothing to say.

'Son, I've brought something to eat', the mother said smiling.

Then the mother opened a packet wrapped in an *Ekkam* leaf. They were cooked rice with a strong aroma. She then again took out a half burnt bamboo piece. Narmi wondered what might be the content! But to his surprise, Narmi found the bamboo piece filled with fish roasted and smoked in fire place. The last item was even more interesting. They were powdered chillies mixed with dried chopped bamboo shoot and *Eso* meat. Looking at Narmi the mother said in a manner of explanation.

'This, we call *Luktir* in Galo'.

'Have you ever tasted?, the mother asked with a curious eye.

'No!', said Narmi shaking his head.

Karik and Karie laughed and Narmi joined them with a broad smile. Narmi almost released a drop of water from his mouth looking at the ethnic Galo delicacy. Finally the mother served and they had their meal together, all four of them. Narmi had his belly full. He wanted to take more but his stomach didn't permit him. He never had such a satisfying meal even in his whole life. It was like dream to him; sitting together and having meal with such a loving mother. After the meal they had a few chitchat about the school, friends and food served to them. And then, after sometime the mother expressed her willingness to leave as she was already late. The happy family reunion ended very soon. Karik became quiet and the mother became serious sensing the time flying fast. Narmi stood aside without a word and Karie seemed quite carefree and casual. Finally, while moving out of the hostel the mother said with a heavy heart, hiding her tears.

'Study well. Don't quarrel and fight with friends'.

She gave a hug to Karik and then waving good bye to Narmi walked away. Narmi envied that hug from the mother. He stared at them and almost a tear rolled down from his cheek. Narmi also fell in love with Galo recipes and though young discovered that the Galos are fantastic cook. He also started fantasizing about Karie. To him, Karie was a beautiful specimen of female animal. Her long straight hair, beautiful smile, innocent yet charming attitude left a permanent impression on Narmi's mind.

That day Narmi had a troublesome night. He spent the night rolling from one edge of the bed to another. A feeling of hollowness swept over him. He missed his late mother. He missed his sister Neyang and brother Nai who was far, far away from him. He wanted someone to love him like Karik's mother. His mind was occupied with thousand thoughts and so sleep didn't come to him easily. But when ultimately sleep came he had a dream. In his dream, he and brother Nai were angling in a river. Narmi caught three big white fishes and he was proudly displaying it to his sister Neyang who was standing in the other side of the bank. Getting up early, as usual he went to the school and attended his classes. That afternoon Takeng came running to him with a parcel and an envelope. They were addressed to Narmi and they had stamp and seal which clearly indicated the dates. Narmi was shocked to see something addressed to him. With a trembling hand he received the packet and the envelope and out of curiosity he rushed to a corner and tore open the packet. It was a beautiful sweater, hand knitted by his sister Neyang. He also tore the envelope and went through the content of the letter.

Dear Narmi,

'Hope this letter finds you in sound health and happiness. I'm fine here and your younger brother Nai is also fine. Be strong physically and mentally. Study hard and focus on your ambition. Don't spend much of your time in playing and don't argue with your friends.'

The most surprising fact about the letter was that, inside the letter Narmi found a 30 rupees note wrapped carefully in a corner. Neyang wrote…

'I'm sending only rupees thirty. This is all I have. Spend judiciously. Buy a pen or a copy. I'll send more if ever get a chance.'

Yours
Mem Neyang

Narmi was in the seventh heaven. Thirty rupees was a huge amount for a boy like him. And for that sweater Narmi was full of gratitude to his sister as winter was nearing. He felt as if god had sent that sweater for him with a blessing. Thus Neyang was always there through thick and thin. She was the only hope and the standing pole where Narmi could lean upon. The same evening at 4 p.m. taking permission from the hostel warden Mr.Pradhan, Narmi along with Takeng and Taking went to the market. They had sweet Rasgollas and Narmi also bought some pencils and Camlin water colours. He was happy at least for the time being though it didn't last for long.

Growing up at BKMS for Narmi was a mixture of innocence sprinkled with little bits of joy, sorrows and bitter experiences. But the most important part on the way of his growing up was that he became a determined person. He started to dream. But it wasn't a mere dream, he wanted to hunt them. BKMS had a great result every year and it produced many bright students. Thus BKMS, became a popular 'trademark' in the field of education. Rich envied this orphanage and many of them wanted to push their children into BKMS. This let many well-to-do parents to produce fake orphan certificates in order to get their ward admitted to BKMS. Thus some years later the presence of rich in the cradle of poor diluted the atmosphere of BKMS.

Being with friends, living like a family under the same roof; and under the influence of routine works and busy schedule Narmi never knew how the years rolled. Surrounded by many good friends like Micky from Tarak, Aten from Karko, Joluk from Kambang and Rijum from Daporijo, Narmi could never measure the pace of time. The only thing he hated most was the 45 days vacation period where he had to separate himself from his friends and teachers. But Narmi had his own explanation for that. Boys with at least single parents surviving; father or either mother, were the most fortunate and happiest one. They could at least enjoy a warm well come home at their arrival and have a satisfying bite of fowl or chicken to quench their love for meat. But for Narmi, it was the most gruelling hour of his life and he hated that at any rate. Various thoughts would come to him at the commencement of vacation period. 'Where would I go?', 'How would I spend the 45 day break?', 'Who would be there when I arrive?'. Of course a house for namesake was there, where Nai stayed with an old acquaintance who was appointed by the villagers. His was a mere presence, without any moral and emotional support and on the other hand, Neyang had left her studies and she was almost like a bird; feeding herself and doing all sorts of odd job to support her two little brothers. Though young she was strong and determined. She had already taken a vow that she would never let her brothers down or let them beg before anyone.

Narmi had his bitterest vacation once when he was in the standard seven. Micky, who grew to be one of his best friends came to the bus stand to see off his friend who was leaving for his village. Seeing Talen and Talung, who were from the same village he said.

'Talen, stay around Narmi!'

'You belong to the same village', Micky said giving some stress.

'You needn't worry when I'm there!', Talen replied with a smile.

'When is the bus coming?', Micky asked.

'May be at around nine I suppose', Talen replied.

'It starts from Yingkiong', Talung added.

After sometime the boys had a sight of the rickety state transport bus. It arrived Boleng giving a long, high pitch deafening horn. Even before the driver put his brake, there were swarms of people rushing towards the bus. Like Narmi, there were many boys and girls from BKMS who were going for the vacation. When the bus finally stopped, Narmi along with Talen and Talung rushed into the bus pulling and pushing. The seats were all covered. It was hard even to keep ones' leg in a stable position. The middle spaces between passenger seats were also full of goods and human feet. Narmi's trunk was left with Micky who was still standing below.

'I'm keeping your trunk in the hood Narmi', Micky said lifting the heavy trunk.

'Ok, keep it in a safe place. Be careful', Narmi cried out from inside.

'Boys, happy journey! We'll meet again', Micky yelled.

'We'll be back again!', replied the boys in unison from inside.

The bus was fully packed and Narmi was struggling with all his might. He was almost squeezed and flattened and he was finding it hard even to breathe. While in the process of getting himself adjusted inside Narmi unfortunately was pushed towards someone's armpit. She was a hefty non-tribal woman whose armpit gave such a strong foul smell that Narmi almost vomited. In order to get fresh air, Narmi stretched his neck like a crane to avoid suffocation. The roof of the bus was equally crowded with humans and goods heaped in an unorganized manner. Though the conductor was yelling using abusive words nobody cared him. More and more people were climbing up, and some were dangling in the rear ladder of the bus. The man ultimately gave up, blew his whistle and the bus rolled on with a loud roar and hiss. Narmi waved his hands out; his body and face still struck inside the bus. Standing still, Micky and other boys waved back.

After a long struggle of negotiation with sharp turns and winding trails the bus finally reached Pasighat. It was a tedious and sluggish journey. Narmi, having the sight of Dangaria Baba temple was the most excited. He had a sigh of relief seeing Pasighat again after a long period. He could now breathe freely. Reminiscence of good old days was pouring into him. Talen and Talung were equally excited when the bus got them to State Transport Station. Narmi quickly got down from the bus, as he was a bit worried about his trunk. He hadn't seen Micky putting the trunk on the hood of the bus. The conductor was already there, helping and putting the luggage down. Narmi, quite agitated called the conductor.

'Conductor, please put my trunk down'

'How do I locate?, There are so many!', the conductor replied in a busy tone.

'It has my name. Narmi, BKMS', replied Narmi looking up.

'There is no trunk by such name!', the man said after scrounging.

'No trunk by such name! How come?'

'Micky said he would keep the trunk up', murmured Narmi.

Talen and Talung had already collected their trunks and were helping the conductor in locating him. They too were shocked to learn that the box was really missing. Narmi was worried and tormented. He didn't believe and thought it shouldn't be true.

'Please…check it again!', Narmi repeated with stress.

'My boy, I promise. I've already checked', the man replied irritated.

Narmi almost collapsed and cried. His clothes, pants and shorts, vests, towel and the Bible were all gone. How could he ever stay without these spare clothes? Thinking so, Narmi started sobbing bitterly. Talen and Talung tried their best to console their friend but the situation was out of control. But after half an hour, he finally got under control and all three of them walked towards the Public bus stand. They had to catch yet another bus that leads them to Ruksin.

At the station, Talung felt around his pocket and said cheerfully.

'Boys lets have *Pan*!'

'Betel nuts are costly. Do you have money?', Narmi asked.

'Yes! Why not?', Talung proudly displayed a ten rupee note.

'Yeah! Lets go!', Talen almost dragged Talung.

Coming to a *Pan shop* Talung ordered the shopkeeper to prepare three *Pan*.

'Please prepare three pan for us. One zarda, and two meetha pan'

The shopkeeper within a minute prepared the *Pan* as directed and handed it over to the boys.

'How much?', asked Talung boldly.

'Six rupees', Answered the shopkeeper smiling.

After giving the money and getting the change, Talung offered the *Meetha Pan* to Narmi and Talen. He took the *Zarda Pan*. Talung, opening his mouth wide threw the *Zarda Pan* into his mouth and started to chew the junk like a cow. He swallowed the flavor and let them run down his neck and stomach. Talen and Narmi did the same with the *Meetha Pan* stuff. But their junk stuff was quite sweet and had an enjoyable flavor. However a change came over Talung, after a minute of chewing the *Pan*. He started to feel a sizzling burning sensation around his mouth. He was also getting dizzy and his head ached. Then to Narmi and Talung's surprise, Talung started to vomit vigorously. Holding his head, he was throwing spit everywhere. Collapsing on the ground, he shamelessly cried.

'My head is spinning around!'

'Aya, get me some water!', Talung said waving his hand around.

Talen rushed to a nearby canteen and collected a bottle of water. He then dragged Talung to a nearby tree shade. He sprinkled water to his face and head and let him to drink some water. Talung washed his face and took some rest beneath the tree. Talung actually was ignorant about the content of the *Zarda Pan*. It was a traditional Indian *Zarda Pan*, a junk stuff consisting of ingredients like…betel nuts, coconut pieces, sweet stuffs, and most importantly tobacco powders. After fifteen minutes Talung stood up, still holding his head. In a trembling tone, he said with a shy smile.

'I thought it would taste good'

'How come you know about *Zarda Pan*?', Talen asked laughing.

'From my uncle', Talung replied laughing back.

'I think we should avoid such useless stuff!', Narmi said with a mood of persuation.

'Why didn't you warn us earlier?', Talen said and three of them burst into laughter.

Then there came the shrill whistle in the air. The bus started roaring, the front engine chamber shaking briskly and smokes coming out from silencer with a loud purring sound. The boys rushed back into the bus with their belongings and the bus rolled towards Ruksin. Later that evening Narmi had a cold reception. The old man in charge of Nai had no reaction. He was not at all interested about Narmi's home coming. But at least Nai was the most excited seeing his elder brother, back home. He felt a soldier returning back home after spending half of his life at country border. But Nai was shocked to find Narmi returning empty handed.

'Where's your bag?', Nai breathed.

'You didn't bring anything for me this time?', he added.

'I was bringing some marbles for you!', Narmi said silently looking aside.

'Where is it? Where is it?', Nai cried excitedly.

'I lost everything!', Narmi replied looking down.

'Are you serious? Not kidding?', Nai asked looking straight into the brother's face.

'Someone picked it up', Narmi replied in a low tone.

'Let the rascals hands and feet rote', Nai said in great anger.

'How did he dare to grab someone's belongings!', he added.

'Well, your presence is more important to me than anything else', Narmi said smiling.

'Come, I'll tell you many things about BKMS', he added hugging his little brother.

Thus the brothers spent the night happily though without a fowl or a chicken. Narmi shared his experiences and told his little brother about his improvements and desire to study more and more. Next day, the brothers went to a nearby river and took bath. Narmi was good at swimming. He demonstrated his little brother, how to wave his arm and trash his legs and keep afloat. Narmi, a grown up now was in shorts while bathing and Nai naked. Narmi also washed his only shirt as it was full of dirt because of the previous day journey. After bathing they went back home. Narmi left his only shirt to dry in the *Tunggo*, a raised platform at the entrance of every tribal hut. Half naked he and Nai went inside to have their midday meal of rice and mustard leaves with non iodine salt. Nai being a fast eater left the plate early, Narmi still crouching with the lump of tasteless rice. Nai all of a sudden called out to Narmi in the top of his voice who was still with the unfinished plate.

'*Babing..Babing,* a cow is chewing your shirt!', Nai cried agitated.

'Hus…hus…the bastard! Evil takes you away!', Nai cried again in a loud voice.

The cow was still there chewing the cloth firmly; jaws moving up and down, full of white foam coming out from her wide mouth. Narmi rushed out in a hurry taking broad steps throwing his rice plate to a corner. He jumped down from the *Tunggo*, picked a long stick and gave a repeated lash to the cow. The cow ran away leaving behind the half eaten cloth. Narmi grabbed the cloth and tried to spread the shirt. But he had a worsening sight. The shirt was now full of little holes and it almost became a rag. Narmi almost cried and said helplessly.

'What shall I put on now?', Narmi murmured.

'Hell takes away the evil cow!', Nai said in great anger.

'Would I be without clothes? What would the people say?', Narmi questioned himself.

'May be you can try mine', Nai said in a patronizing tone.

Then Narmi and Nai lay down near the entrance, gazing at the roof. Narmi was in his short, half naked. Closing his eyes, he pondered. Various thoughts came to his mind. He thought about his lost trunk, of his late mother and about his sister Neyang who was everything for them. After remaining silent for a while, he breathed.

'Where's Mem now?', Narmi asked in a low tone.

'Itanagar', Nai replied.

'With whom she is staying?', Narmi asked again.

'With an uncle', Nai replied.

While laying down Narmi's eye gave a prolong itch which he had to rub repeatedly. His *sixth sense* told that his sister was coming very soon. Then Narmi had a seeming voice of his sister echoing in the air. He thought that it was a mere imagination going inside his mind. But a little later a voice was really heard in the air. Narmi and Nai turned and had a look towards the direction of the sound. To their utter shock and surprise they saw their sister really appearing from a corner, smiling and calling.

'Nai…Narmi….I have come back!'

Narmi couldn't believe his eyes. His heart began thumping and he prayed God again and again. Nai on the other hand was extremely happy to see his elder sister back home. He ran and hugged the sister and Narmi took the bag from Neyang and together they stepped towards the house. Narmi grew emotional and started crying. Neyang too was sobbing, shedding many drops of tears holding her brother. On the other hand, Nai the youngest was confused at the unique family reunion seeing them crying. He was rather impatient and restless expecting she might have brought sweet with her. A little later, Neyang rubbing her tears said.

'Why need to cry? We should be happy!'

'I have come a long way from Itanagar'

'Where is Itanagar?', Nai asked innocently.

'It's far..far away! You cannot imagine.', explained Neyang.

'Well...I'll tell you about Itanagar in the evening. Now let's have sweet', she added opening her bag.

Neyang unzipped the bag and Nai was the most curious. For him it was something wrapped in wonder. Narmi too was curious but being the elder brother, he had that patience. Neyang took out a packet of cashew nut for her brothers and some sweets. Nai was already watering in the mouth and was ready to have the bite. After the sweet, there was yet another surprise for the two little brothers. Neyang took out another packet, wrapped beautifully. It was a bigger surprise for the boys...shorts and shirts for each of them. Narmi considered himself the happiest man on earth seeing the gift.

'Nai, I won't be naked now!', Narmi said looking at Nai.

'Yes! Of course', Nai replied.

'Naked! What do you mean?', Neyang asked in confusion.

'Mem.. he lost his belongings', Nai reported looking towards the sister.

'May be somebody has stolen it', Narmi said in a low tone.

'You should always be careful!', the sister advised.

'Well, I'm not worried now', said Narmi thanking his sister immensely.

Then the three of them laughed together. Neyang felt a strong inner satisfaction seeing her younger brothers in happy mood. It was one of their happiest hours and Neyang wanted it to happen in that way only. She had been away to Itanagar; the capital of the state, looking out for greener pastures, to support herself and her brothers. Though hardly eighteen, time had taught many things and she was learning through her experiences. Each obstacle was a new lesson to her and she had to pass through each of them without looking back. And yes, she was fortunate. At Itanagar, she met one of her old uncle Taying, who himself was doing a small job in a government establishment. He knew Neyang, loved her like his own kid and hence supported and encouraged her in many ways. Uncle Taying was one of her strength and she began to look life with lots of optimism. It was because of Taying that she got absorbed as casual employee in an office and started earning a bit. It met her little demands and she now could look after her two little brothers. That night they slept together, Neyang in the middle like a mother and the two brothers lying beside her. She like a mother was narrating them about Itanagar.

'Where's Itanagar Mem?', Narmi asked out of curiosity.

'It's far…far away, about 300 kilometers!', Neyang replied.

'How big is the town?', Nai asked.

'It's very big, bigger than even our Pasighat!', Neyang said seriously.

'There are so many huge buildings. It's crowded with people from different places. There are so many beautiful shops and you will find almost everything! The streets are crowded with people and cars of different sizes. There is the Ganga Lake, zoo, I.G. Park, Gompa and most importantly the Itafort!', Neyang elaborated.

Narmi listened to the whole narration in rapt attention while Nai was already asleep. It was already 8 p.m. time for the villagers to slip under their quilts. Narmi in his turn revealed his sister about the hostel atrocities and nightmares. But he also shared his sister about the brighter side of BKMS and his improvements in studies and fine arts. Neyang was happy at this and advised Narmi to keep up the spirit and never let her expectation go down. Then under the dim kerosene lamp they went on to a deep long sleep till dawn. Thus Narmi, being together with his little bro and Neyang didn't know how the time passed. Neyang would keep herself busy in weaving traditional *Gale*, a cloth wrapped around the waist and would sell them to meet her small demands. The brothers would spend most of their day in the field and sometimes would go to jungles with catapult in hand hitting birds. Sometimes they would spend their day fishing in the nearby river that flows through the village.

One day there was a surprise visit by Talen and Oyi, Talen's elder sister. They came smiling and Narmi was happy to see his friend again.

'When did you come Neyang?', Oyi asked.

'I heard these days you're in Itanagar', she added looking curious and smiling.

'Yes Mem', Neyang replied smiling back.

'Got a job?', Oyi asked again.

'Eh! Job of a casual labour!', Neyang replied with a shrug and grinned.

'Let it be! No matter how small the job may be. You're earning, self dependent! That's important!', Oyi said appreciating her.

'Well, I want to know when Narmi is leaving', Oyi said.

'Vacation is almost over!', she added blinking her eye.

'May be in a day or two', Neyang replied.

'I thought of sending the boys together', Oyi said.

'That sounds great. It would be better', Neyang said feeling delighted.

Fixing a day, Oyi and Talen went away. Neyang was happy at the decision of sending the boys together as thing would be easier working with a senior like Oyi. Nai over heard the discussion that went between the elders and felt a deep emptiness around. He thought he would be alone again without Narmi and he knew Neyang would proceed to Itanagar again. Yai, the old relative with whom they were staying was quite old to be bank upon.

On the appointed day Nai sensing his brother was leaving and would be away for a long time started crying and shedding tears profusely. He cried falling down on the ground and kicking his legs in the air. It took time to console him and make him quiet. Neyang like a mother knew how to handle the situation. She opened her purse and slipped a five rupee coin into Nai's pocket.

'Go…get some marbles and sweets', Neyang said pulling him up.

'Don't be rigid. You're a good boy. I'll take you to Itanagar very soon!', she added.

After getting tips from his sister Narmi came back to normalcy. He also voluntarily reduced the loudness of his cry. He instead patted and wished Narmi a happy journey.

'Come back soon brother!', Nai said clinging to Narmi's arm.

'I'll, my bro!', Narmi replied in a grave tone.

Then all four of them; Neyang, Narmi, Oyi and Talen left Rayang for Pasighat boarding a bus at Ruksin. They spent a night at Pasighat in Tatong's residence who was a close acquaintance of Oyi. Getting up, the next morning Neyang and Oyi escorted the boys to State Transport Station with their bags. They booked two tickets for the boys and gave them 75 rupees each. 75 rupees was meant for the whole year and it was a huge sum for Narmi. He could spend that for those items which were not supplied by the school. Previously whenever Narmi had to depart from his sister he used to cry a lot and it was really a hard time for him. But this time he was happy being with Talen. And more over this time his pockets were hot. He had many things to do with that, buy a book, a pen or a pencil of his choice or throw a treat to his friends. Neyang was worried sending these under aged boys alone in a bus which would climb rugged terrain mountains full of sharp turns and curls for the next five or six hours of tedious journey.

Back to the school, the boys got themselves mingled with their daily routine. Narmi surrounded by hectic schedules never knew the passing of time. He spent seven long years at BKMS. He was now a teenager, young and ambitious and there came a lot of changes in his outlook and personality. BKMS too was changing. Though the school was primarily an orphanage, later it was crowded with rich children. Thus the whole atmosphere got diluted and the hard earned fame was tarnishing day by day. Disciplines among the students got deteriorated and the relationship between the teachers and students were getting sour. BKMS was almost going to collapse and many of the good teachers were disappearing day by day. The message, that BKMS would become a pay school and would remain no more an orphanage worsened the boys. This very message spread among the boys and girl dormitory like a wild fire and Narmi was the most worried.

'I heard, we'll have to pay from the coming session', Narmi told Taking almost whispering in the ear.

'Me too, but not so sure', Taking replied shrugging his shoulder.

'If we really need to pay I'll quit the school', Takong said in a serious tone.

'Why need to pay? This is an orphanage!', Otin said almost in anger.

'Orphange! There are so many rich boys around!', Taling said with contempt.

'How did they get in?', Narmi asked turning to the boys.

'God knows! Ask the principal and the teachers', Taking said.

There was a silence in the air. Narmi sat in his bed, legs swinging. The boys like scavengers perched together discussing the burning issue. It was a casual discussion but a genuine issue to ponder upon. It could destroy the career and hope of so many orphans. Narmi became grave and muttered.

'If I have to pay I too will quit the school'

'How can I afford?', Narmi added feeling hopeless.

'I'll also quit', a voice echoed from Tamar.

Just then there was the sound of heavy stumping coming from outside. The boys sensing the Captain, scattered and hurried away to their seats.

'What were you doing boys?', Tani asked with a crooked smile.

'Nothing Captain. Just chatting, being Sunday', Taking answered who was the boldest among the boys.

Then there was the sound of the midday meal and the boys rushed towards the dining hall taking their plates. Momar stumbled against a boulder, fell down and broke one of his front teeth. He stood there, blood flowing out from the gums but nobody attended him. It was like a mad race, a stampede and survival of the fittest. Narmi was a part of this race. It was in his eighth year at BKMS, Narmi got a shocking letter. It read...

*'Narmi, there are things which can't be hidden.
I'm now married to a stranger. He is from Runne
village. Address him as Big brother. But don't worry,
I promise to stand by your side. Nai is with me now.
He has been admitted to a primary school and is
doing good. Study hard and be sincere, if you want
a space for yourself in the society'.*

Neyang

These lines were a big blow to Narmi. His was a mixture of reaction. He was certainly worried but at the same time he was happy too. He was worried thinking that he won't be able to claim Neyang purely as his own. He thought that she belonged to someone now. He was happy in a sense that someone has been added to their small family. That night Narmi kept thinking; his mind wandering from one corner to another. There was no coherence in his thinking; it skipped from one end to another. At the same time he was really curious to know about the new member in the family of three. He murmured.

'Who could this man be?'

'How might he look?'

'Would he support me and Nai?', Narmi questioned himself.

Yes, Narmi had the chance to see this man very soon. BKMS was to become a pay school as the authorities were facing heavy financial crisis. No aid was coming from any corner, neither from the government nor from any private individual or NGOs. The school was coming to a near closure and the situation was growing worse especially for real orphans like Narmi. There was a growing fear among the orphans that they will have to leave the school by themselves before the school kicks them out. Narmi was mentally prepared to leave the school after his final exam as he knew his Neyang wouldn't be able to bear the expenses with her meagre salary.

One day a man came looking for Narmi just after he attended his standard ninth final exam. He had short stature, having a harsh and rude voice. Narmi soon came to know it was Tarak, his brother-in-law. He had come to take Narmi out of the school. They went to the Principal's office and completed all the official formalities. Mr. Rao the Principal, while handing over the School Leaving Certificate to Tarak said.

'We are helpless! We too are servants. We work under the direction of the higher authorities'.

'There are so many like Narmi who are quitting the school', he added in a low voice.

'What will be the future of these boys?', Mr. Rao murmured to himself looking aside.

Tarak seated in front of the Principal didn't say anything. Then Mr. Rao, turning to Narmi said.

'Narmi, you have been a good student throughout and I hope that you keep up this spirit where ever you go!'

'Be smart and studious'

'Our blessings will be with you always', Mr. Rao gave his last advice.

Narmi then went to the hostel to pack up his belongings as he had to leave Boleng the next day. Climbing up the hill top, Narmi took a heavy sigh and then he stood still like a statue. He looked down, gazing the Boleng town, scattered with huts and few government buildings. He then looked down again at the school building, then to the play ground where he used to play. He stood there, as if he wanted to fix everything into his mind before leaving BKMS. Narmi was solemn and grave and he didn't speak to Tarak, his brother-in-law for few minutes. Tarak understood the situation and respected Narmi's feelings. So he was calm and quiet and didn't pass any comment on Narmi. But as Narmi turned towards the hostel to collect his beddings, he saw an army of friends coming to see him. They knew why he was leaving the school and so nobody dared to ask the reason.

'Heard you're going to continue your studies in Itanagar!', Aten said smiling.

'Yes, may be. My elder sister is there', Narmi replied calmly.

'Wah! You're so lucky!', exclaimed Karik.

'I'm afraid whether I'd be fortunate enough to visit Itanagar or not!', Takong said, his words almost inaudible.

'I'm also planning to pursue my high school at Itanagar!', Micky said confidently.

'That would be great!', Narmi said.

'I'll also study at Pasighat from the coming session', a voice echoed from Taking.

'I don't have any plans right now', Karik said.

'I think Itanagar would be better than our BKMS', said Aten.

'Why not! It's the capital!', said Rijum standing at a distance.

Then more and more friends gathered. There came Joluk, Talen, Taling, Raje, Tadu, Tayop and Marge. They were to see Narmi for the last time as he was leaving the school permanently. There were many like Narmi who were leaving the school. Boys from affluent families had no reaction at such farewells but only the unfortunates like Narmi suffered. Getting emotional Narmi almost dropped a tear but he stealthily rubbed them looking aside and gathering some strength breathed.

'Boys, I'm leaving but I promise to write you back!'

'Don't forget us!', said Karik in a loud voice.

'Okay! Bye', Narmi cried back.

Micky gave his last hug, followed by Talen and many others. It was a memorable moment to be cherished especially when one is alone and Narmi knew he was going to miss them.

'I'm joining you in Itanagar very soon!', Micky said to comfort his friend.

'Me too!', Aten said with a smile.

'Bye! See you soon!', Narmi cried back, lifting his beddings.

Tarak and Narmi then taking long steps stepped away from BKMS. A lot of questions arose in Narmi's mind while walking. He didn't know where he was heading. He didn't know whether the path he was following was right or wrong. He was confused and muddle head taking an unknown decision. They took shelter for the night at Mrs. Yamang's house, an old acquaintance of Narmi; to leave for Pasighat the next morning. Lying down with folded hands Narmi's mind was occupied with old BKMS reminiscence and a confused future. He didn't know what exactly he needed to do. But on the other hand he was happy too. Itanagar has been a dream for Narmi. He fantasized about the city and had a long standing desire to visit the city. He was not satisfied with the mere verbal description given by his sister Neyang. He wanted to go there and see things for himself practically.

CHAPTER SIX

IN THE CAPITAL

Fortunately destiny takes Narmi to the state capital Itanagar, some 300 odd kilometers away from Rayang. Nai was already there at Itanagar and Narmi was impatient to meet his younger brother after a long time. Narmi now smiled to himself, hoping at the scope of seeing Itanagar, the city of his dream. Fixing a day Tarak and Narmi headed for Itanagar. They boarded the state transport bus at Ruksin check post, the state boundary between Assam and Arunachal. Narmi excited and with a gleam on his face rushed into the bus and occupied the window side; his favorite seat. He felt as if the whole city was waiting for him with its arms wide open and Narmi wanted to grab this chance. He had many dreams, hope and aspirations looming before his eyes. They appeared before his eyes like a mirage but he wanted to hunt and follow them at any rate.

After the regular police checking at the gate, the bus rolled towards crowded Jonai. Jonai as usual, was crowded with people, rikshaw pullers, sweet meat sellers, shops, stray dogs and cattle and the place polluted by the craws from crows. It was going to be Narmi's second longest journey in life and he was finding it quite thrilling; it was not like his previous experience. Travelling in the *Adi Among* was tiresome and monotonous. The jerk was almost nil and the seats were comfortable. It wasn't a crowded bus unlike the hill bus. Everyone had a seat and well accommodated. Narmi looking out from the window enjoyed the scenic beauty of Assam plains. The vast green meadows that spreaded like sheets many kilometers away enchanted Narmi the most. He wanted to get down and roam about idly, in the open space in full freedom swinging his arms. He wanted to dive into and get himself lost in the beauty of the nature if ever he could. Lost in thought Narmi fell into a deep sleep until his brother-in-law woke him up at Dhemaji.

'Narmi wake up, wake up, we are in Dhemaji', Tarak said shaking his shoulder.

'What? Dhema! What's up big bro?', asked Narmi almost half asleep.

'We have reached Dhemaji. Let's get down', Tarak repeated.

'Is this Itanagar?', Narmi asked again waking up from a deep slumber.

'Stupid! This is Dhemaji! Passengers take their lunch here', said Tarak in a rude voice.

'Oh', said Narmi and followed his brother-in-law.

Tarak led him to a road side restaurant. At the entrance sat a dark skinned shabby looking man in vest, preparing roti and poori. He was drenched with sweat because of the blazing stove and his hands moving like the tongs of a machine. At the right corner sat a pot bellied man collecting cash from the customers. Narmi followed Tarak through a narrow and dark room where all the passengers from Pasighat were having their lunch. There was hustle and bustle inside the single roomed restaurant. Many passengers were taking their meal like hungry dogs that had not eaten for a long time.

'Eh, baity! Bath anibi', Tarak called out for two plates of rice in broken Assamese.

The boys were running here and there attending the customers. Some were with plates of rice and yet others with bowls of chicken, fish and mutton curries. It was noisy inside, so the boys couldn't hear what Tarak had said.

'Baity! Baath dibi na. Huni pua nai neki?', Tarak said in a louder voice almost getting angry.

A boy rushed in again to attend Tarak and Narmi with plates of rice and said.

'Huni pua nai na!', the boy replied that he didn't hear.

'Ki mangcho kabho?', a boy with bowls of different meat asked Tarak.

'Murgi', Tarak said chicken.

Then Tarak and Narmi finally got their meal after a long struggle. Tarak within no time completed the plate of rice but Narmi almost hesitated and took the rice half heartedly. It was not to Narmi's taste and seeing the place quite untidy and dirty he couldn't swallow the food served. Narmi's nostril almost swelled up because of the foul smell and stinky human piss coming from everywhere. He got up leaving the unfinished plate of rice. Getting up Tarak paid the bill and went outside. After few minutes the bus conductor blew his whistle and the passengers got in one after another. As Narmi was about to climb the stairs of the bus he was stopped by an old, shabby looking man with a walking stick in his hand. He was crawling with his hands and feet, and stopped Narmi.

'Baabu, baabu, garib par daya karo!', the man said to have mercy on the poor with folded hands.

'Baabu…baabu!', the man repeated almost pulling Narmi in a helpless tone.

Narmi was almost about to set his right leg on the stair but his second thought stopped him. With hesitation, Narmi pulled his leg back to the ground. He stood there perplex and stared back at the crippled old man in rags, who appeared like a mad man. Narmi's instant reaction was to get rid of the old chap but he gave a second thought. He realized his own condition of being poor and helpless.

So he pulled out a ten rupee note given by his brother-in-law and handed it over to the man. Then old man almost snatched the note giving Narmi a crooked look with folded palm and waving his hands repeatedly. Narmi then climbed up the stairs and occupied his seat. The driver then gave a loud deafening horn and all the passengers boarded again into the bus. Tarak too came in chewing betel nut. The bus then rolled on. Narmi's eyes were on the old crippled man and his heart was full of mercy for him. But as the bus gained speed, the man jumped up waving his stick and almost dancing. Narmi was dumb founded and speechless. He couldn't believe what he had seen. The man whom he thought to be helpless and cripple stood up and danced waving his stick!

'Big bro, big bro! look! Look!', cried Narmi looking out from the window.

'What?', Tarak said casually.

'Look! Look at that man! I thought he was cripple', Narmi said taking a heavy breath.

'So what?', Tarak said again.

'I gave him ten rupees!', Narmi said almost in a confused state.

Tarak was silent for a while. But after a second he burst out into frenzy laughter.

'Ha! Ha! Hah! You've been fooled!', Tarak said laughing.

'Stupid, that was a fake beggar!', Tarak said again looking at Narmi.

'Fake beggar! What's that?', Narmi asked still confused.

'You've been fooled man! He is well bodied!', Tarak replied laughing.

'They are shameless and notorious. You must be careful!', Tarak advised Narmi.

Narmi remained silent for a while. He didn't believe what he saw. He had never seen anything like this before. He didn't know the meaning of beggar even. He realized that there are no beggars and cheaters in his own state. They may be poor but they are hard working and they don't cheat others for livelihood. Narmi knew that he was fooled but he learnt a lesson that he ought to be alert at every step.

'Why did he do that?', Narmi questioned Tarak.

'He is too old for that mischievous act!', he murmured looking out.

'They are lazy and they don't have self respect', Tarak said looking at Narmi.

'There are many if you go out of our state', he added and cautioned Narmi to be careful.

The bus sped towards the crowded Lakhimpur. Narmi had not seen so much of people in his life. The driver slowed down the speed because of heavy traffic and Narmi felt that he was sitting on a crawling tortoise. He felt a kind of suffocation and started to feel dizzy. Narmi almost vomited seeing the human population and he wanted to get out of that place as early as possible.

'How far is Itanagar from here?', Narmi asked Tarak again.

'It will take us yet another two hours', replied Tarak.

The bus finally reached Banderdewa and Narmi was very excited. CRPF jawans did their regular Inner Line Permit checking and let the bus roll in. Narmi's face beamed up when Tarak told him that they are already in the capital. As already written before hand, Neyang and Nai was already there waiting for them at C sector Itanagar. It was already 3 p.m. and Narmi was terribly hungry. Neyang, a young mother of a baby daughter was standing there giving Narmi a wide smile. Narmi was so excited to see his sister and little bro after a long interval of time. Narmi also peeped into and had a look at his baby niece for the first time. After the short family courtesy they walked towards Neyang's small quarter.

'Come Narmi, welcome to my bunglow!', Neyang said smiling in a lighter vein.

'The rooms are very small! But don't worry', she added.

Narmi went round the quarter and found that it was a two bedded quarter with attached kitchen and bath room. At the back side was a small extended room where Nai had his bed.

'Abu! Wash your hands and feet', Neyang said to her husband Tarak.

'Narmi, you also!', she added looking at her brother.

'You might be hungry', she said again placing two plates on a table.

'Yes Mem, I'm terribly hungry', Narmi said touching his belly.

Nai was left with the baby while Neyang was busy serving food to Tarak and Narmi. Narmi now ate with full satisfaction though there was no chicken or pork. Neyang stood there by the side of her husband like a typical Indian bahoo or daughter-in-law. After having his meal Narmi rushed into the next room to see his baby niece. She was extremely pretty little baby, fair in complexion and having bright eyes. She almost looked like a little angel, sleeping in a cradle.

'Oh, my god! Pretty little thing!'

'Where did you come from?',

'You're a little angel sent from heavens above!', Narmi sang praising his little niece.

Neyang and Nai began to laugh hearing Narmi singing a lullaby for the first time. Tarak, the father also joined appreciating the baby by giving her thousand different names.

'Have you named her?', asked Narmi taking the baby in his arm.

'Yes, we call her Ponung', answered Neyang.

'It's a lovely name!', Narmi said.

'Let me, let me…can I have my baby?'

'Come my little angel. Come my sweet little honey candy!', Tarak said extending his hands and almost snatching the baby from Narmi.

Next day Narmi got up early and Nai took him for morning walk to Indira Gandhi Park. As they were strolling Nai explained taking his brother around the park like a professional guide.

'It's a beautiful park'

'All the important functions are held here', Nai said.

'What sorts of functions?', asked Narmi with a curious look.

'Eh…26th January, 15th August, Trade Fairs and much more!', replied Nai.

'There is also a old wrecked plane for public display', Nai said pointing a direction.

'Is it?', Narmi asked out of excitement.

Nai took Narmi around the park and using his finger tips gave him a rough idea about the place and their names. Words like Mowb 2, Niti Vihar, Ganga, C sector, and P sector confused Narmi and he failed to remember them all. There after Nai went on explaining about the places of tourist interests like Ganga Lake, Itafort, and the Gompa. Narmi longed to visit them. As they walked along Narmi's love for the city was growing larger and deeper. Clusters of government office buildings and quarters charmed Narmi. He hadn't seen so much of RCC structures in his life. Even the sight of cars and motors filled Narmi's heart with great excitement. He fancied them and wanted to have them. These feelings brought changes in his personality in the later part of his life.

After sometime it was decided that Narmi should be admitted to Government Higher Secondary school, Itanagar. Getting up early, one day Neyang said.

'Narmi, dress up. We need to visit the Principal'

'Where?', Narmi asked looking confused.

'Mowb 2', replied Neyang.

Neyang first took Narmi to Mrs. Yater. She was an acquaintance of Mr. Sharma, the Principal of GHSS, Itanagar. Yater had a telephonic conversation with Mr. Sharma and thus Narmi's admission was done on the other day. Narmi started going to school and became a regular student. He met many new friends like Sanjay, Shovan, Tarung, Bamang and Gumjum. As he was soft spoken and somber by nature friendship didn't come to him easily like others. Narmi had to choose them almost by the process of filtering. Of course he took time but they were the best of his time.

One day as Narmi and Gumjum were walking towards the school Gumjum introduced yet another friend to Narmi.

'Narmi, he is also from Pasighat side', Gumjum introduced Atai while walking briskly.

'Hi, I'm Atai. I'm from Kemi', Atai said extending his hand with a smile that revealed his dimple.

'I'm Narmi. I'm from Rayang village', Narmi replied smiling back.

'You're in which standard?', asked Atai.

'We're in standard nine, section C', Gumjum replied instead of Narmi being outspoken.

As they walked along the pavement, Gumjum's sight fell on a non-tribal motor cycle rider who had a dark skin.

'Where do this black skinned people get these bikes?', Gumjum breathed in a jocose manner.

Then three of them fell into a feat of laughter. Gumjum was an ambitious boy who hailed from Daporijo, Upper Siang district.

'Where do you stay?', asked Atai to Narmi.

'C sector, near I.G.Park with my elder sister and brother-in-law', replied Narmi.

'I'm in D sector, with my aunt and uncle', said Atai.

It was already 9, the school bell could be heard from a distance and three of them had to broaden their foot step and hurried towards the school. As usual Narmi met his class friends like Sanjay and Shovan. Sanjay, whose parents are from Kathihar, Bihar was a studious boy who always used to carry a dictionary in his hand. He knew almost all the words of Oxford mini dictionary and hence friends addressed him as 'Walking Dictionary'. Shovan, son of a DSP was a brilliant student who came from Chandranagar, Itanagar. Both these boys were a source of inspiration for Narmi. Though he was a mediocre student, seeing Sanjay and Shovan he became a book worm and spent most of his time in studies.

One evening Atai came looking for Narmi and proposed him for a short stroll at I.G. Park. Narmi without any hesitation, obliged the request and headed towards the park. IG Park, an open space filled with fresh air was the only spot in Itanagar where one could enjoy and be at peace remaining away from the maddening world. Exchange of views and sharing of opinions brought Narmi closer to Atai. He found that Atai also belonged to a humble family and so like him; he too was a practical man who remained aloof from worldly pleasures. Thus bit by bit there formed a good chemistry between the two, which resulted into a strong bond. That evening Narmi introduced his friend to Neyang.

'Mem, this is Atai from Kemi', Narmi introduced.

'Where do you stay?', asked Neyang.

'In D sector, with my aunt and uncle', Atai replied.

After a few gossiping Atai expressed his willingness to leave as darkness was spreading fast. But as he was about to leave Neyang said.

'Why, what's up? So early?',

'You have come to our place for the first time. You'll have your supper here', said Neyang.

'We have chicken today!', Narmi added.

'well, then I won't decline', Atai said shyly with a smile.

'Actually Mem, my aunt is quite strict', said Atai laughing.

'That's good! But you'll have dinner with us today!'

'Okay, I'll speak to your aunt if necessary', said Neyang looking at Atai.

So Atai had a sumptuous meal that evening with Narmi and his family. He appreciated the meat prepared with bamboo shoot and made some charming remarks that made the whole family laugh. And this way Atai was successful in curving a niche with Narmi and his family. They would go to school together and would return from school together and thus their friendship grew inch by inch.

One day Narmi came to Atai's place with a poem composed by him with the title, *'Nature's Beauty'*. Atai went through the lines and praised immensely.

'Why don't you try it for a publish in the local dailies?', asked Atai.

'How do I do that?', asked Narmi with curiosity.

'Okay boy, I'll', replied Atai and they posted the article to *'The Arunachal Times'*, a leading local dailies.

Narmi forgot to check the dailies as he was busy with his daily chores of studying, listening to music and attending petty house hold works. Sometimes he also used to look after his baby niece when Neyang and Tarak were busy and occupied. One afternoon, after the school hour Gumjum had a surprise visit to Narmi. He had a copy of *The Arunachal Times*.

'Wow! You're a poet man!', Gumjum said appreciating Narmi.

'I was just going through the lines…and happened to see your article!', he added.

'Where?', asked Narmi almost snatching the paper from his friend.

Narmi saw his poem titled *'Nature's Beauty'*, beautifully printed among the Poetry section of the paper and was extremely happy. He rushed in, and showed it to Neyang who appreciated in big terms. These little words of praises injected Narmi and roused his jotting habit and his spirit of composition whenever he was free. The next day, Narmi almost became a hero in his class. Words of appreciation flowed and many friends congratulated him seeing his poem published in an esteemed daily. Shovan was the most influenced.

'You're brilliant man! You're a true poet!', said Shovan seriously.

'You've a good vocabulary too', he added.

'You've a multifaceted quality boy!', Sanjay said loudly.

'No man. Not in the least!', said Narmi.

'I'm a jack of all trades and master of none!', said Narmi looking around to his friends.

'No, I don't agree that', said Shovan protestingly.

After the school, Shovan took Narmi to his place. Mr. Adhikari, the DSP too was impressed by boy's work. He being a B.A. (Hons) in English was much more interested into poems than his own son Shovan. He went through the poem thrice and encouraged Narmi to come up with some more.

It was already 2 p.m. time for lunch. While placing the plates on the table Shovan's mother said.

'Son, you must have informed of your arrival',

'I'd have prepared some good dish', said Mrs. Adhikari smiling.

But Narmi was a bit confused to see many colorful food items placed on the table. There were many bowls of different sizes and smokes coming from them were giving a beautiful smell. Along with the plates of rice were the bowls of dal, potato fried with ladies finger, round boiled egg fried with onions and garlic, a plate of papad and a bottle of mixed pickles. But the most beautiful was the big bowl, which contained spicy fish curry kept somewhat at a distance. The beautiful smell coming from the big hot case was irresistible. Narmi's mouth began watering even before the food was served. Mrs. Adhikari served the plates of rice and then went on to put the vegetables one after another. Then in a loving voice she said.

'Son, you can have your meal now!'

'This is your home. Be free and donot hesitate', she said with a smile.

Narmi started taking the food along with Shovan. The beautiful aroma coming from the various bowls doubled Narmi's hunger and the different colors of the food items mesmerized him. He had seen such colorful food items only in the magazines and in the Hindi movies. Watching them before his eyes and having a taste of them was something which he couldn't believe. The mother standing near but not very close to them was attending the boys. Her hand moved from one item to another. Sometimes she would lift a papad and place on Narmi's plate and sometimes with a spoon of fried potato with ladies finger. But the bowl of spicy fish curry was not touched. It still lay at a corner. Shovan was having his meal quietly and busy chewing firmly without a complaint and comment. Narmi's eyes were on the big bowl but he thought *a beggar cannot be a chooser*. He thought of extending his hand for the fish curry but he had to resist his temptations and listened to his conscience. Narmi was about to finish his plate but the spicy fish curry was not served. He wondered why. His mind was boggling and a lot of questions came to his mind. He wanted to know why the fish curry was not served yet! He thought if Mrs. Adhikari had not been there he would have grab hold of the bowl and devour them in one single bite. But to his dismay she was still there standing and smiling. Narmi would often stealthily lift his face and have a look at the bowl and at Shovan. He was restless inside but he pretended to be at calm. He gazed at his friend who ate without a complaint and Narmi wondered why! But as Narmi was about to give a finishing touch to the remaining 20 percent of the content of his plate, Mrs. Adhikari stepped up and said while lifting up the big bowl containing fish curry.

'Now boys, try this fish curry prepared in a typical Bengali style!'

'Narmi do you want some more rice?', she asked while putting the fish curry into Narmi's plate.

'Oh! No. Thank you!', said Narmi.

'My stomach is already full!', added Narmi.

Narmi wanted to say 'why didn't you serve the fish curry earlier?' But it got chocked somewhere in his throat.

'Why? Young boys should eat more!', Mrs. Adhikari said smiling in a funny way.

Narmi finally had the fish curry, it was incredible and he would have asked for some more rice if it had been served earlier. He wanted to have more of it but his stomach didn't permit him. There were no space left in his stomach and he had to finally quit the table. Later that evening, Shovan dropped Narmi at C sector in his dad's Maruti Gypsy. Though they belonged to two distinct societies, time had brought them closer to each other like the minute and hour hands of a watch.

'Thank you man!', said Narmi while getting down from the vehicle.

'Thanks! For what?', asked Shovan with his eye brow raised.

'It's a part of my duty', he added smiling.

'Whenever you feel like visiting me, give me a call', Shovan said again while giving his number.

'Thanks friend', responded Narmi.

Then Shovan started the vehicle and rolled away waving good bye to his friend. But as Narmi was about to put his leg to the entrance door he heard a noisy quarrel inside. He didn't expect it would be his elder sister and his brother-in-law. Seconds later he could again hear the sound of empty vessel thrown against the wall. Then, came the ugly sound of another empty steel tumbler rolling on the floor. They were deafening and torturing. Narmi stood there, silent and still. He became serious and could hear his own heart thumping. Nai was standing somewhere in a corner. Stark terror had seized him and his legs were almost shaking.

'What's this fuck about?', asked Narmi stepping towards Nai.

'Are they arguing again?', he asked again feeling agitated.

'Yes!', replied Nai in a whisper.

Nai scared as a rat while Narmi was disturbed and tortured. He wanted to know the reasons behind these quarrels. He could hear his sister brooding and weeping in a corner of the room and Tarak, the brother-in-law was throwing volleys of abusive words to Neyang.

'You dirty lecherous woman!'

'How dare you to say that?', said Tarak in a loud and harsh voice.

Ponung who was just three years old was under the arm of domestic maid and crying bitterly. Narmi was confused and didn't know how to react. He picked his baby niece and patted lovingly but she didn't stop crying. Tarak, slamming the door went outside with heavy steps without even looking at Nai and Narmi. After some time leaving the baby to the maid, Narmi and Nai went to their room to study. Narmi wanted to go inside and have a look at his sister but he couldn't gather any courage. He wanted to tear apart Tarak or anyone who touched his sister but he was too young for that and at the same time he thought he had no full claim over Neyang. She was now somebody's wife. This made Narmi to take any concrete decision and come to a legitimate solution. Narmi as usual was sitting there with a book but his mind was somewhere else. Nai was almost asleep, nodding. Neyang slowly appeared from a corner, holding her waist. Her hairs were shabby and she spoke to Narmi in a very painful voice.

'Narmi, where did you go today?'

'I think you were late', she said but smiling trying to hide the pain.

'Oh, I've been to one of my friend's house', replied Narmi in a low tone.

'To talkative Sanjay?', asked Neyang in an amusing manner.

'No. Shovan, the DSP's son', answered Narmi.

'What happened Mem?'

'Why did you argue?', asked Narmi unable to remain at calm.

'On petty domestic matters', replied the sister and started weeping again.

Narmi became emotional and started to cry along with his sister. Nai who was sleeping short while ago also began to sob seeing Neyang and Narmi. But Neyang being the eldest, rubbed out her tears and said smiling.

'Why should we cry for?'

'We're nobody's slave!', said Neyang trying to make bold his younger brothers.

She then looked again at Narmi and said in a very sweet tone, as if a mother advising her child.

'See Narmi, such things happens in life'

'There are moments of sad and joy. Nobody can predict future and nobody is perfect'

'These are small, small things that comes in our lives. We should be positive in all aspects and hope for a better future!'

'Your only job is to study! If you want to be someone!', Neyang advised Narmi and Nai.

Narmi and Nai listened to all these advices silently without a single word of interruption and with great concentration. Without her nobody had a word to them as they were alone, and Narmi knew each and every word that flowed out from his sister's mouth were as precious as a gem. And then to cheer up her brothers Neyang said.

'We have chicken today! Come on boys, let's have our dinner', Neyang said smiling.

'Is it? Really?', Nai asked.

'Yes, but artificial one!', replied Neyang laughing.

'What?', Nai asked in confusion.

'We have Nutrella, soyabean!', said Neyang laughing loudly and all three of them laughed together in chorus.

The journey doesn't stop here. Noisy arguments and sometimes a little bit of fighting between the heads of the family were not an obstacle on Narmi's way. He used to go to the mother's lap, at IG Park and study there beneath the shade of the pine trees and study peacefully. His efforts were fruitful and he passed many of his exams with flying colors. He smiled to himself at his success but yet they were more satisfying.

'Congratulations Narmi, you're in the third position I suppose!', said Sanjay extending his hand for a shake.

'Yes', said Narmi smiling back.

'You scored the highest in English man! Congrats!', said Shovan hand shaking Narmi.

'Is it, I didn't check', replied Narmi.

Then Gumjum started counting the boys who would be opting for science stream. Like a priest he was chanting the names of studious boys one after another.

'Shisangka, Shovan, Narmi, Atai, Pritam, Amit, Tarung, Bamang and Sanjay…'

'I'm not opting science. I prefer Humanities!', said Narmi looking at his friends.

'Me too!', added Shovan seriously.

'Why? Why?...', asked Sanjay shocked.

'I have my own reasons', replied Narmi.

'Me too, but my dad insists me to opt Humanities', Shovan said.

'What has happened to these boys?', said Sanjay seriously.

'Let it be arts or science, eh! It makes no difference'

'Only thing is that you need to be good and hard working', Gumjum said.

'Yes of course!', Atai commented.

Narmi actually had his own dream. He too was interested in Science like the rest of the boys. But he knew well his economic background. Opting Science would need him a lot of money and he knew his sister wouldn't afford that any more. She now had become a mother of two and had her own responsibilities. This discouraged Narmi to think even of Science and made him mentally prepared for Humanities. Thus within two years Narmi cleared his High school along with Shovan, Atai, Gumjum and Sanjay. On the day of the CBSE result Narmi along with his many friends had enjoyed Samosas and cold drinks at Aakash Deep Complex. He was happy at his own success but there was none to share them with. At noon Narmi returned to their quarter along with Atai. He was extremely happy and wanted to share them with Neyang and Nai.

'How is your result Narmi?', Neyang asked impatiently on seeing Narmi.

'Pass', replied Narmi with a broad smile.

'In top second class Mem', added Atai

'Really? That's great!', exclaimed Neyang with great excitement.

'Did you hear Abu?', said Neyang turning to her husband who showed a cold response.

'Oh! thank you, God. My brother will be in college now!', said Neyang again almost with a tear in her eye.

Tarak had no interest in Narmi's result. He took it casually and didn't show any reaction. After remaining silent for a while he said rather in a discouraging manner.

'That's not a big deal'

'Everyone pass class twelve!', said Tarak almost with a contempt.

'Eh! You're a class twelve fail', gave Neyang a bitter reply.

This remark made the boys to laugh at Tarak. Nai who was still struggling in standard five also started laughing with his big brothers. Neyang out of excitement almost forgot to enquire about Atai's result.

'Well, how's your result Atai?', she asked lately.

'45% in aggregate Mem', replied Atai with a smile.

'Good', said Neyang.

'Take this, celebrate at your success', said Neyang slipping rupees 300 notes into Narmi's pocket.

'Thank you Mem', said Narmi in great excitement.

'Abu, why don't you go to the market and get a big hen?', said Neyang looking at Tarak.

'Yes, your highness!', said Tarak with a grin.

After sometime Narmi and Atai along with little brother Nai went to Bank Tinali and had a coffee and some Chinese dish in a restaurant. They also visited the Gompa and the state museum. Altogether it was a great day for Narmi. In the evening they had a small party completed with chickens and mutton. Tarak the brother-in-law, though harsh and rude by nature was an excellent cook. His chicken and mutton curry let Atai to suck his fingers even after he finished his plate.

That very night Narmi couldn't sleep. His mind kept on wandering from one thought to another. He was impatient to know how college life would be. He knew he would do Honors in English, his favorite subject. He then thought of his desire to become a college lecturer. Though ambitious sometimes he was a bit pessimistic about his dream. With his eyes closed, he would see his future bright and sometimes bleak. But he thought he wouldn't look back once he had decided whether he succeeds or not.

The next day as Atai and Narmi were having a stroll at IG Park, they met Gumjum and Bamang. As they walked they started talking about their future plans.

'Narmi, what's your plan?'

'I'm planning to go to Delhi', said Gumjum enthusiastically.

'I.., I've no plan'

'I'll be here only, at Dera Natung Government college', replied Narmi in a low voice.

'You should be in a good college', said Gumjum again.

'College doesn't matter! Study matters', Atai interrupted.

'Yes, but the taste of being in Delhi itself would be different', Gumjum replied.

'Where are you planning Atai?', asked Gumjum again.

'I'm planning to go to Cotton college Guwahati, Assam'

'But if situation favors only!', replied Atai cleverly in order to pull down Gumjum's bossy nature.

'We are leaving next week', said Bamang who came from an affluent family.

While walking idly Narmi's mind wondered. He too wanted to go outside his state and study somewhere. But he could do that only in his dreams. Whenever such thoughts came to him Narmi hated himself and his fate. So he had to give up such thoughts and led a very practical life. In the evening Shovan came to Narmi and told that he was going to Delhi the next day.

'Have you chosen the college?', Narmi asked.

'Not yet'

'But I'm planning to go to Delhi University or either to Hindu college', answered Shovan.

'But I shall be missing you!', said Shovan looking grave.

'Don't worry, we shall be in touch!', said Narmi.

Shovan didn't ask about the college Narmi was intending to join; for he knew about his friend's position. Narmi envied many of his friends going outside the state for further studies. But he had no choice and had to satisfy himself with the lines spoken by Atai that ran *'College doesn't matter. Study matters!'*. After few days Narmi along with Atai got his admission at DNGC. Narmi also met many new friends at the college campus, like Yajum, Sumi, Hidam and Monica who later became very good friends to him. Though Narmi had been in Itanagar for the last four years, he had not seen DNGC. The college's Administrative building, Academic blocks, the beautifully structured Library building, the huge Auditorium attracted Narmi so much that he forgot Shovan's DU and Kirnya's

St. Edmunds college, Shillong. What he hated about the college was the College canteen and the rickety college bus driven by Saikia. Otherwise it would be a perfect place for learning, ideally located, away from the city and the crowds.

Narmi enthusiastically attended his classes at the college. Walking almost 2 miles from C sector to DNGC on foot and that's too on stone pavements didn't worry him. It was really a fun to walk to college with friends like Yajum, Hidam, Atai, and Sanjay. Sanjay would talk restless picking up various topics and Yajum had to stop him blocking her ears with her palm.

'Can't you shut up your mouth?', said Yajum.

'Why? Why do you curtail the freedom of expression?', replied Sanjay laughing.

'Yes, I'm with Sanjay', said Atai who had a bit of Sanjay element.

'If he does not talk, we may be late for the college!', said Atai looking at Yajum.

'Why?', asked Hidam confused.

'How far is our college from Ganga and C sector?', asked Atai.

'Almost 2 miles, I suppose', answered Hidam.

'Yes! That's the point. We would be tired walking on foot', said Atai.

'His talk diverts our mind from these ugly slippery pebbles', said Atai again.

'Yes of course! But he is also quite informative', said Narmi supporting Sanjay.

'Yes! At least, I've someone in my support!', said Sanjay loudly staring at the two girls.

'Anyway no talk please. We have reached the college!', Yajum said while walking away briskly.

Yajum and Hidam ran to attend their Education lectures while Sanjay hurried away for Political Science, and Narmi and Atai headed towards the English Department. Dr. Khan was already doing *'To his coy mistress'*, by *Andrew Marvell*. Dr. Khan's eloquence and impressive interpretation of the poem enticed Narmi thoroughly. He would sometimes imitate his style and now so his desire to become a college lecturer was even greater.

After the class Narmi met Tujum, who hailed from Along, West Siang District and who became a good friend.

'Hi, Narmi. How are you?', Tujum asked seeing Narmi.

'I'm fine. Thank you', Narmi replied smiling back.

'Come! Let's go to the canteen', Tujum proposed.

'This is Atai. We are in the same department', introduced Narmi.

'Hi', said Atai.

They walked into the little crowded canteen. Sanu, a boy of 14 was busy attending the customers. Though illiterate, he was agile as a horse and friendly to everyone who came to that canteen.

'Sanu, serve us the hottest item in your canteen', Tujum placed his order.

'The hottest item right now is the frying fan!', replied Sanu in a jesting voice.

Everyone inside the canteen began to laugh and Tujum himself couldn't control his urge to laugh. But he said.

'Non-sense, I didn't mean the frying fan. You eat your frying fan!'

'Bring us tea and samosas', Tujum ordered.

Tujum paid the bill and they came out of the canteen.

'Oh! Do you know tomorrow is Freshers meet?', Tujum asked raising his brows.

'Is it?', Atai asked.

'Yes'

'Grab the chance to see beautiful girls!', Tujum said smiling sitting on his Yamaha RX 100.

'Okay. I won't miss!', said Narmi nodding his head and walked to his friends.

The next day Narmi also geared up for the Freshers meet. He ironed his old pant and put on a new shirt gifted to him by Neyang. He went to Bank Tinali in order to catch the bus early for getting a seat. When the bus arrived, he boarded the bus and got a seat next to a girl. He didn't feel comfortable sitting next to an unknown opposite sex. So he avoided looking straight into the girl's face and wouldn't talk unless she did. But the girl seemed free and confident.

'Are you new to the college?', she asked turning to Narmi.

'Yes', replied Narmi.

'In which department?', she asked again with a smile.

'English', replied Narmi again.

'That sounds great! English is tough', said the girl.

'Anyway...I'm Sunita. I'm in geography 1st year', said the girl looking bold.

'Call me Narmi', Narmi said looking into Sunita's face.

'Where did you do your schooling?', asked Narmi.

'Don Bosco, Lakhimpur', Sunita replied.

'Why DNGC then?', asked Narmi with a curious look in his eyes.

'It's better than Assam in many ways', replied Sunita in a carefree manner.

The bus reached Ganga. There were many students still to board the bus though it was already crowded. Within no time Narmi grew free and confident. He looked straight into Sunita's face whenever they talked. She had put on a maroon colored churidhar and a matching dupatta. She was pretty, and her voice was charming. Seeing the hand bag and her heel Narmi guessed she belonged to an affluent family. The crowded bus finally got the college campus and Narmi had to get down.

'If you don't mind, stay with me for sometime!'

'I've no friend. Would you?', Sunita insisted.

'Why not! Come!', said Narmi boldly and they stepped towards the academic blocks.

'Today is Fresher's day. Do you know?', asked Narmi.

'Oh, really?', Sunita asked with surprise.

'Yes! And you will be asked to sing', Narmi said laughing.

'Don't lie. You're just kidding me boy!', said Sunita slapping him on the shoulder.

As they walked towards the auditorium, Narmi met Tujum, Atai, Yajum and Hidam. Seeing Narmi with an unknown girl for the first time, Yajum waved her hand gesturing who the girl was without uttering a word. Narmi simply had to smile back as there were many students outside the auditorium. They went inside and occupied seats for themselves. Narmi looked around and saw many hundred students crowding the auditorium. There were students from every district of Arunachal such as Adi, Apatani, Galo, Nyishi, Nocte, Wancho, Tagin and Mompa. Many were from Assam and other parts of India. Narmi wondered what Fresher's day was all about and everyone inside the hall was curious and impatient.

The programme began with a beautiful folk dance presented by the senior students of History department. Mr. Tayu, Lecturer from Political Science department was hosting the programme. He was a product of JNU New Delhi; young, smart and handsome. All the girls' eyes were on him and Narmi looked at him with an envious eye. He informed the Freshers that there would be introduction and question rounds for the selection of Mr. and Miss. Fresher. After a minute, students started coming on the stage one after another as directed by the host. A boy came up first.

'My name is Nabam Tam. I'm from Sagali'

'Why did you join this college?', asked the first judge.

'I've no choice. There is no college in Sagali', the boy answered innocently.

The audience laughed at Tam's response and Mr. Tayu called for the next Fresher.

'My name is Karoty. I did my schooling from Government Higher Secondary school Pasighat'

'I want to become a Social worker', the girl added boldly.

'Why did you join DNGC?', the second judge asked.

'For better exposure. Actually, I wanted to go to Delhi but my percentage is low', the girl replied.

'Next', the host said loudly and a boy came up.

'I'm Marnya. I'm from Along, West Siang district'

'Why this college?', the third judge asked the same question.

'My parents can't afford me outside', the boy replied.

'What do you want to be?', the first judge asked.

'Administrative officer', the boy said.

'Very good!'

'Next!', Mr. Tayu announced again.

Now it was Narmi's turn. He was 65 in the line. Seeing the hall packed and sensing thousand eyes on him, Narmi trembled from top to bottom. He almost lost his confidence but he tried to be bold before the audience. Seeing the Principal, Lecturers and Professors seated in rows and thousand students staring at him, he almost collapsed but somehow managed to stand straight.

'Your good name please!', the first judge said.

'I'm Narmi. I did my schooling from Government higher secondary school Itanagar', answered Narmi.

'Why did you decide to join this college?', the fourth judge asked.

Narmi was a bit confused though he had heard many responses from previous students. He wanted to say he couldn't afford or something, but that too didn't come out from his mouth. He stood there for a second, thinking and ultimately remembered Atai's line.

'College doesn't matter. Study matters!', he said.

'DNGC is no less than any other college in India. It's a privilege for me to study here'

'Why should we go outside when we have it here?', he asked the audience loudly.

The audience roared out, clapped and many students whistled in the air. Narmi came down the stage and sat with Sunita. But Narmi was confused. It seemed to him that the judges were not satisfied with his answer for they didn't react at all.

'Well spoken!', said Tujum.

'Yes, I think you gave an excellent response to that non-sense question', Atai added.

Sunita simply smiled looking at Narmi. There were more than 250 freshers who came from different schools and districts of Arunachal and who belonged to different tribes and family backgrounds. The whole drama lasted for more than three hours. In order to kill the audience's monotony senior students of the college presented various cultural items. After the introduction round, Mr. Tayu the host announced.

'Attention please!'

'The judges are now furnishing the results. Let's see who will be the Mr. and Miss Fresher of this college!'

'Are you ready? Curious to know?', Mr. Tayu asked the audience.

'Yes! Yes!', the crowd hauled like foxes again.

Prof. Sharma, the principal of the college spoke on the occasion. But he had to cut short his speech seeing the students impatient to hear the result. After the speech, a judge came up and handled a piece of paper to Mr. Tayu, the host. The crowd became silent and began to hold their breath.

'Are you ready guys?', Mr. Tayu cried loudly.

'Yes!', the crowd responded excitedly.

'So, here's the result…'

'Mr. Fresher…goes to, Narmi!', the host cried to the audience.

'Wow!', the hall echoed with whistle.

'And, Miss. Fresher…goes to Miss. Gebimang!'

'Wow! Wow!', there was a blast in the air.

Atai jumped up and lifted Narmi in the air out of excitement. Sunita and Tujum congratulated him immensely. Yajum and Hidam came struggling from a corner and shook hands with Narmi. Mr. and Miss Fresher were called to the stage and everyone's eyes were on them. Narmi almost became the center of attraction especially among the girls who stared at him. Narmi received a Packet wrapped beautifully in a colored paper and a certificate of commendation. With trembling hand Narmi received the prize from the principal of the college. Waving his hand to the crowd Narmi climbed down the stage and the audience responded with deafening clap.

'You have to throw a party Narmi', said Tujum.

'Yes! Yes!', said Yajum and Hidam.

'It's not a big win', said Narmi.

'Why not? You've been picked out of so many students', said Sanjay.

Out of pressure Narmi felt his pocket and found only a 20 rupee wrinkled note. He wanted to enjoy the moment with his friend but he felt helpless and miserable. 20 rupees won't serve his purpose as there were many friends. So he had to act clever in order to avoid disgrace.

'Let's see tomorrow! It's too late now', said Narmi turning to his friends.

'Yeah it's okay. Let's see tomorrow', said Atai reading Narmi's face.

It was already 4 p.m. Narmi along with his friends rushed to the rickety college bus to occupy seat. Narmi got one but sacrificed it to his new friend Sunita, who thanked him with a broad smile. When Narmi got his quarter, Nai and Neyang were already there. Neyang was busy feeding the second baby nephew and Nai sitting idle. Narmi with the prize of the day appeared from a distance smiling.

'What's up bro? You're smiling to yourself?', Nai asked seeing his elder brother.

'Yes, see this!', said Narmi displaying the wrapped packet and certificate in his hand.

'What's that?', asked Neyang curiously.

'I'm selected Mr. Fresher of the college today!', announced Narmi proudly.

'Is it? Really?', asked Neyang excitedly.

'Yes, see this!', said Narmi showing his certificate.

'Very good! Keep it up', said Neyang with great happiness.

Narmi tore open the wrapped packet and found to his surprise that it was a dictionary, Oxford Advanced Learners Dictionary.

'Wow! It's a dictionary!'

'I've been seeing this in the book stores'

'It's very costly. Rupees 700', informed Narmi to his sister.

'It's God's blessing', said Neyang and turned to her youngest brother.

'See Nai, I'm worried about you'

'Your brother is doing well in everything'

'I may not be always with you. I'm married now! You should try to understand', said Neyang in a grave tone.

Nai lowered his head down and listened with attention. He became serious and remained calm without a single word.

'He will be with me later on!', said Narmi seeing Nai a bit depressed.

'That's what I want always. You must always be together!', advised Neyang.

The serious discussion between the brothers and sister was disturbed by the appearance of uncle Taying at the door.

'Oh, it's you uncle. Please come and have a seat', said Neyang smiling.

'Good to see three of you together', said Taying.

'Where's Tarak and Ponung?', asked Taying looking around.

'May be in the park', replied Neyang.

'How's your college Narmi?', asked Taying looking at Narmi.

'Good', replied Narmi.

'He got a prize today', informed Neyang impatiently.

'Very good. Keep it up', advised Taying.

'For Nai I've no words. I'm tired of him', the uncle added.

'What did you win Narmi?', asked the uncle.

'Mr. Fresher, DNGC', answered Narmi showing the prize.

'May God bless you with many more prizes!', prayed the uncle.

Taying pulled out a five hundred rupee note and handed it over to Narmi who received with a trembling hand. Narmi was extremely happy as he had not seen a five hundred rupee note. Neyang who came out from the kitchen with a tea tray saw it and said warningly.

'Don't be a spendthrift! Use that for buying books'

'Mem, friends were asking for a party', said Narmi looking at Neyang to win confidence.

'Today I felt around my pocket and found only a 20 rupee note!'

Hearing this all of them began to laugh but Neyang didn't. She took out her purse and pulled out a 200 hundred rupee note and gave it to Narmi.

'I'm a rich man now with 700 hundred rupees in my pocket!', said Narmi smiling broadly.

'Neyang there is a vacancy of a peon at SC Department. We can apply for Nai 'said Taying sipping his tea.

'Is it', asked Neyang cheered up.

'Drop an application tomorrow itself', Taying suggested.

'Narmi you can draft an application for your brother since you are in college', said Taying turning to Narmi.

'Yes, I would', replied Narmi readily.

After having his tea Taying went away. Narmi and Nai also went to their room. Neyang as usual, leaving the baby to domestic maid kept herself busy with kitchen works.

'I'm happy. I'll work', said Nai looking at his brother.

'I don't like to study. I hate books!', he added looking away from Narmi.

'I know', said Narmi quietly.

'I'll work and support you', Nai said with confidence.

'You must. There is nobody to bank upon', Narmi murmured.

Next day Neyang and her uncle Taying went to the SC department with the application. Taying narrated the Director about the applicant and his condition. The Director was a sympathetic man. He ordered one of his staff to put up the file, but said frankly.

'There is a vacancy. But don't expect a regular post'

'He'll be kept as adhoc', the officer warned.

'Don't cry my daughter. Hope for the best!', the officer said to appease Neyang.

'Run after the file in order to grab the job', Taying suggested while coming out from the office.

'I've done my duty. Now it's yours', he added and went away.

Narmi as usual went to the college. He was greeted by many friends. As promised, he took his friends to the college canteen. But they were stopped by a senior student on the way. He wore a black sun goggle and stepped out from his Maruti 800. Narmi mistook him for a Lecturer but coming near, he extended his hand for a shake.

'I suppose you're Narmi, Mr. Fresher!', the boy said with a weird smile.

'Yes, I'm Narmi', replied Narmi calmly in confusion.

'Congratulation'

'I'm Techi Tam, B.A. 2nd year', the boy made his introduction.

'Last year I lost my vote for the post of General Secretary', he added boastfully.

'This year I'm contesting again!', Tam informed Narmi.

Narmi's confusion was now over. He was no more a school going child and acted cordially.

'Can we be friends?', he asked putting his hand on Narmi's shoulder.

'Why not!', answered Narmi smiling and looking at his friends.

'Let's go to the canteen and have something!', the boy proposed.

'Actually I've a bunch of friends', said Narmi.

'That's no problem', replied Techi Tam carelessly.

'Come my friends, all of you', said Tam taking Narmi's friends into the packed canteen.

Yajum, Hidam, Atai, Tujum, Sanjay and Sunita followed Narmi and his new friend Techi Tam without a word. The girls were timid and hesitant but Tam being outspoken made them laugh with his cranky remarks.

'Hey boy, bring us all the eatables in your canteen!', ordered Tam.

'Okay big bro', Sanu the canteen boy replied.

'Fast! We are hungry terribly!', he said again.

Yajum and Hidam giggled at his remarks and Tam began laughing to himself.

'Friends this small tea party is on behalf of Narmi, Mr. Fresher!', said Tam smiling and looking around.

'Thank you, Tam', said Narmi shyly.

After the tea, Yajum, Hidam and Sunita thanked Tam but he responded diplomatically.

'This party is for Narmi. Give your thanks to him without wasting your time!'

Tam pulled aside Narmi to a corner and said in a whisper.

'Narmi, you're the Mr. Fresher. You must have at least fifty supporters on your side. Please help me out this year. I on my side would extend you all possible help!', said Tam pleadingly.

'Not exactly fifty, but I promise to support you!', replied Narmi quietly.

'Shall I drop you to your place Narmi?', asked Tam.

'Some other day for sure. I've friends now!', replied Narmi and turned to Sunita.

'Huh, where are they?', asked Narmi seeing Sunita alone.

'They already left', replied Sunita smiling.

'Why didn't you?', asked Narmi again.

'Why would I?'

'I'm not like them who leaves a friend behind!', Sunita explained with a smile on her lips.

'Thank you, madam!', replied Narmi smiling back.

'I want to take you to my place today. Would you?', asked Sunita hitting Narmi on his shoulder.

'You needn't give me a fist. I'm ready boss!', replied Narmi laughing.

Sunita took Narmi to her place. She was staying in a small rented house in Ganga. They walked leisurely and no serious discussion went between them. All they talked were on casual topics. Narmi was a bit hesitant walking alone with a girl but he didn't want to hurt Sunita as she became a good friend now.

'Who else stays with you?', asked Narmi.

'I'm all alone! It's such a bore sometimes', said Sunita looking aside.

'I miss my family a lot sometimes', she added.

They got the room. Sunita opened the door and Narmi followed silently. It was a two small room with attached bath and a toilet.

'Oh, It's too hot!', she said while reaching her hand for the fan.

'Come! See my bedroom', said Sunita almost pulling Narmi inside.

'Oh, my God!', cried Sunita picking up her colorful undergarments left scattered on the bed.

Narmi stood there confused and didn't know how to react.

'I was in a hurry this morning and forgot!', said she hiding them in the middle of piled clothes.

'Come, sit here!', said Sunita pushing Narmi to the bed.

'I'll be comfortable in the sitting room', said Narmi hesitantly.

'Are you afraid? I'm not going to eat you!', said Sunita laughing.

'Take this and have a look at them', she said throwing Narmi a bunch of Cosmopolitan magazines.

'Be at ease! I'll take a bath first and prepare meal for us', she said and slipped into the bathroom.

Narmi was there turning to the pages of the magazines. But he failed to concentrate. Something or the other disturbed him. He didn't know the cause of these disturbances. He had never been alone with a girl till now and his conscience too didn't permit him. But he finally realized that Sunita wasn't his beloved and thinking so he tried to be normal and sensible. After 15 minutes, Sunita came out from bath. Her long hairs were still wet and there were water droplets on her shoulder. She had wrapped herself in a soft white towel and she looked very sexy. She sat in a chair adjacent to the bed and started combing her hair looking in a small mirror. She then started painting her lips. Narmi stealthily raised his head and sometimes stared at her. But in the process he was caught ultimately.

'Why don't you look straight into me?', said Sunita with a smile.

'Who's looking at you? I'm reading magazine!', replied Narmi.

'God only knows!', Sunita said laughing.

'You look really pretty today', admired Narmi.

'Is it?', asked Sunita looking straight into Narmi's eye.

'Yes, but I'm terribly hungry', replied Narmi.

'Oh, yes. I forgot', she stood up and looked for her clothes.

'Now, close your eyes boy!', said Sunita from a distance.

'Why man?', asked Narmi as if not knowing.

'You're a boy and I'm a girl. I'm changing clothe', Sunita cried like a little girl.

'Okay madam!', said Narmi closing his eyes with the magazine in his hand.

But Narmi peeped through the edge of the pages and looked at Sunita's bare back. She was really seductive and Narmi thought if it was not him, she would have been an easy prey. But practically Narmi had no courage for he had no previous record or experience. His conscience defeated him every time and he had to act accordingly. After changing her clothes, Sunita started preparing meal for both of them.

'Please help me in cutting the onion Narmi', said Sunita after putting the cooker on the stove.

'I'm going to prepare egg and tomato curry', said she laughing.

'It's faster you know!', she added again smiling.

'Do you cook?', she asked again turning to Narmi.

'Often. It's my elder sister who cooks', replied Narmi rubbing the tears on his eyes.

'Don't cry baby, I'm here!', said she snatching the knife and onions in Narmi's hand.

'I'm not a good cook either. My mom does most of the cooking at home', Sunita said turning quite home sick.

They had their lunch together. The egg and tomato curry was not up to the mark. It had the smell of raw mustard oil but out of hunger Narmi didn't pass any comment to his friend. He simply made an ironical remark.

'You're an excellent cook. I had my belly full', said Narmi holding his stomach.

'Don't try to fool me, I'm not a fool!', said Sunita staring at Narmi.

'It had the smell of raw mustard stupid!', said Sunita and they laugh together.

After the late hour lunch Narmi walked back to his place. Since he was alone, he avoided the high way and followed the narrow lanes in order to cut short and save his time. He was in IG Park for some time thinking about Sunita. But his conscience woke him up again and reminded that he shouldn't deviate himself from the main purpose of his life. Thinking so he hurried to his room.

A week later, Neyang returned from SC Department with an envelope. It was an appointment letter for Nai. She was taking broad steps and seemed restless but excited. Stepping on the door and taking heavy breath she said.

'Nai, you've got the job!'

'I'm so happy. You can join the office from tomorrow', she said with a smile.

'Is it?', said Tarak snatching the appointment letter.

'Good, at least we'll be free from one burden', remarked Tarak.

'What burden? They are my brothers!', said Neyang staring at her husband.

Nai innocently smiled but had no words to thank his elder sister. She was everything for him and elder brother. Nai simply murmured.

'From tomorrow I'm going to office!'

'Yes, I would accompany you to your office on the first day!', said Narmi patronizing.

'Abu, I think we should celebrate this happy moment', urged Neyang.

'My purse is empty!', said Neyang and laughed.

'Oh, here it is', said Narmi pulling out 300 rupees note to Tarak, the brother-in-law.

'Where did you get Narmi?', asked Neyang puzzled.

'Oh, that day my bill was paid by a friend contesting for General Secretary', Narmi told laughing.

'That's great! A friend in need is a friend indeed', said Neyang in a serious tone.

'I'd throw a big party when I draw my first salary', Nai said after remaining silent for a while.

'And would buy new clothes for my son', he added picking up the baby nephew Kaling.

Nai started attending his office from the next day and Narmi, his college. When Narmi reached his college there was hustle and bustle in the college campus. He met Tujum and Atai who informed that college election would be in a week. Girls in tempting get up would roam about idly and boys would follow trying to court them. Free party and free lifts were available here and there to woo voters by the candidates contesting for election. The college canteen was always crowded during the day time and at night parties were held at different spots, sometimes at MLA cottage and sometimes at Mowb 2 or at Chandranagar. Narmi with bunch of friends like Atai, Tujum, Sanjay, Hidam, Yajum, and Sunita would sometimes join day parties thrown by Techi Tam and enjoy free lifts from his Maruti 800 or Gypsy. It used to be a great day for every collegian. Affluent candidates would throw free parties at Akash Deep complex or at Hotel Itafort or at Blue pine. Voters would throng them like crows and scavengers feeding themselves without paying a penny.

'I'm grateful to all the Adi and Galo friends of mine', said Techi Tam at a small pre-election party.

'This party is just the beginning. They are in rows and a grand party is promised if I win', said Tam.

Techi Tam had the introduction from all his invitees and guests and thanked them vehemently for coming to his party. Then all his Nyishi supporters shook their hands with the Adi and Galo students.

'The Adi and Galo are like us! They are straight, faithful and kind hearted', said Miss Yami, a Tam supporter.

'We can be one through all times of need', said Tam in his last speech.

Then there came the loud music played on a system. Boys and girls, many of them intoxicated, swum to the music of *2 Unlimited* and *Vengaboys*. Everyone moved to the music but Narmi and Sunita sat there in a corner. Sunita had a cup of tea and Narmi hesitantly sipping beer.

'Why don't you join the dance!', Sunita asked Narmi jeeringly.

'You go and join…not I', replied Narmi fearing she would really do.

'Have you ever danced, in a party like this?', asked Sunita.

'No, I hate parties and especially dance!', said Narmi looking into Sunita eye.

'But I like it very much! Shall I go and join?', asked Sunita teasingly.

'You fool! Go on…and join', said Narmi squeezing Sunita's ear.

'Ooh, it hurts! You're jealous! Why?', said Sunita laughing.

There was no response from Narmi. But Sunita knew that their friendship was slowly taking a new shape. It was a spontaneous change which needed no explanation. Their eyes gave the clear evidence that they were in love but none of them expressed in audible words.

After an hour the loudness of the music was lowered and Techi Tam addressed the gathering again.

'Friends, this is the beginning of our friendship. It's a long journey, but today we stop here. There are many more such parties in the days to come! And I promise a grand party if I ever win!', Tam repeated in a loud voice.

'Friends if you have any problem come to me. I'm always there for you!', said Tam turning to the Adi boys.

'Good night and bye!', said he and the party ended.

It was only 7 p.m. The party didn't last long. Narmi as usual escorted Sunita to her place but this time he didn't enter her room as he was already late.

The college election took after a week. The campus was worth seeing crowded with students and vehicles. It was almost like parliamentary or assembly election. Cars, buses and other means of transportations were made available to the voters on the very day. Narmi along with many of his friends enjoyed to and fro free lifts on the voting day and casted his vote. He stayed in the campus along with many friends till 5 p.m. waiting for the declaration of results. After a long wait, the result was announced in a loud speaker and Techi Tam was declared the winner. His supporters jumped up and lifted Tam in the air hawling.

'Hurrah, Techi Tam long live! Techi Tam long live!', cried his supporters.

Then there came the whooping sound of the motorcycles. Boys accelerated their motorcycles to display smokes around them followed by shrill horn of motorcycles and cars. Narmi along with many of his friends rushed to Tam and congratulated him. Tam was excited beyond the limit and shook hands with his supporters.

'Friends, a grand party is welcoming you tomorrow at MLA cottage, from 7 p.m. onwards!', cried Tam in a loud voice.

———◆———

The next day at 6 p.m. Narmi along with Atai walked to Ganga to pick up Sunita. He had no particular dress code for the party, but put on what he thought was the best.

'Get dressed up madam! We're here to pick you', said Narmi.

'You must escort me back after the party!'

'Or else I'll kill you boy!', said Sunita warningly.

'Of course he would', said Atai in Narmi's favor.

'Hurry up! It's already 6.50 p.m.', said Narmi.

'It takes time for me to dress up! I'm a girl, and don't be so excited. Party wouldn't run away from us', said Sunita laughing.

'Yes, of course! Take your time', said Atai smiling.

Sunita went inside her bed room to change her dress. Narmi was curious and impatient of her return. He wondered what dress she would put on. Finally after 15 minutes Sunita appeared. She had put on a fitting white T-shirt and a blue jean pant and a matching scarf. Her dress was simple but she looked very charming and exotic. Narmi was truly impressed.

'So, can we move now?', Narmi asked staring at Sunita.

'Yes your highness!', replied Sunita laughing and looking at Atai.

Then three of them walked towards MLA cottage, where the party was being held. The party could be heard even from a good distance. A fusion of music, shrill cries and booming sound of motorcycles was heard even before they reached the main gate. At the gate Techi Tam along with five or six friends was giving a formal reception. Tam wore a coat suit and a matching necktie, which gave him a look of some executive or officer.

'Good evening and welcome to my victory party!', Tam said shaking hands with Narmi and his friend.

'Sunita, don't leave the party early huh!', he added excitedly.

'Congrats Tam!', said Sunita shyly and followed Narmi.

Narmi along with Atai and Sunita occupied a table. He was shocked to see so many Techi Tam supporters. Some were busy drinking, some sat in groups and yet others loitering here and there without any specific direction. A deafening music was coming somewhere from a corner and so it was almost impossible to hear what the other was saying. Three smart looking girls appeared before Narmi and asked.

'Wow, Mr. Fresher? What would you prefer?'

'Whisky, beer, or local wine?', asked the first girl bending low to Narmi's ear.

'Beer', said Narmi hesitantly looking at Sunita.

'I prefer whisky!', said Atai and extended his hand quickly.

'Won't you take Miss, friend?', asked the other girl to Sunita.

'Do you serve tea?', asked Sunita.

'Tea? No tea! This is no tea party!', replied the girl laughing.

'OK. I shall bring Pepsi for you', said the other girl humbly.

'Pepsi in a victory party? No way!', commented Atai looking at the serving girl who looked quite hot and sexy.

Then a group of girls came again with a tray of mutton, chicken and pork curries and yet another girl with a basket of fried fish. They were wrapped beautifully in *Ekkam* leaves. Tam made his round to every table and corner of the party and said.

'Friends, drink and eat as much as you can! Enjoy yourself but no fight please!'

'This party is thrown just for you. To everyone who loves me!', added Tam.

'One more peg please!', said Atai to the girl server taking four peg in a row.

'You're still with the second glass?', he said laughing.

'No, this is the third!', lied Narmi blinking Sunita.

Narmi wasn't used to drinking but for the sake of party he didn't deny the offer. Sunita on the other hand was still sipping her glass of Pepsi.

'Excuse me love birds! Be here, I'm joining Yajum and Hidam', said Atai and went away stumbling. He got a bit tipsy and couldn't maintain his balance. There were Yajum, Hidam, Tujum, Monica, and Yale who were already dancing to the tune of music played loudly. It was like a free style dance bar. Some were popping and locking, shaking and still others trembling out of cold. It was an amusing scene. Narmi and Sunita laughed to each other seeing it. Many of them being tipsy, were unstable and failed to maintain balance and were almost fumbling. Tujum stealthily came from a corner and dragged Narmi and Sunita.

'So what are you doing guys?', said Tujum while dragging Narmi and Sunita.

'Oh, no. I can't dance, I can't dance', Sunita cried.

'Oh, my God! Dance, and me?', asked Narmi to Yajum.

'So, do you think we are good dancers?', asked Atai pushing Narmi and Sunita from the back.

Narmi and Sunita had to give up their protest and join their friends. Narmi moved his hands and feet clumsily in an awkward way. Sunita who knew a little bit of dancing saw Narmi and started laughing hysterically. And in the meantime, Atung a second year B.A. student came and started dancing in front of Sunita. Narmi couldn't bear this and went aside. He stood there in a dark corner disturbed and tormented mentally. Sunita after a minute came looking for him and found him.

'Why? Narmi? What's up?', she said coming near. Narmi didn't answer.

'Why? That boy came and, how could I stop...?', said Sunita pleadingly.

Narmi paid a deaf ear and remained silent.

'I'm leaving, you stay back', said Narmi with a change of tone.

'So, are you jealous? I don't recognize him even!', said Sunita in a low voice.

'Let's leave, I don't like this party', said Sunita pulling Narmi.

'That would be better', replied Narmi and followed Sunita.

It was already 11.50 p.m. Narmi and Sunita stealthily escaped from the party. They were walking side by side. Being mid night, the temperature had fallen and Narmi wanted to put his hand on Sunita's shoulder. But he had no courage at all and at the same time they were just friends, not lovers. After 20 minutes they reached the room.

'Oh, I must take bath before going to bed', said Sunita.

'Now?', asked Narmi confused.

'Yes, I'm feeling a bit uneasy. Sweats!', replied Sunita looking at Narmi.

'I'm feeling dizzy and sleepy too!', said Narmi.

'Why don't you take a bath? Or fresh up yourself!', Sunita urged.

'Take this! Go first', said Sunita throwing Narmi a soft towel.

Narmi went inside and took a naked bath. With the towel wrapped around he came out after 5 minutes.

'So fast? But, thank you!', said Sunita and went inside to take her time.

Narmi sat there, waiting for Sunita's return. He was a bit worried and confused. He could't decide, whether to leave or stay back with Sunita as it was already past twelve. Sunita came out after 15 minutes, wrapping herself with a white towel around her bosom. Narmi sat on her bed crossed legged. He was still in a towel and vest. Though sleepy he observed Sunita stealthily and examined her. She was rubbing her hair using a small hand towel and then started combing her long straight hair. She looked beautiful and gorgeous. The water droplets on her shoulder made her look sexy and seductive. Narmi wanted to enjoy the moment fully but he knowingly asked.

'Shall I leave now madam?', he asked.

'Are you crazy? It's past twelve'

'I don't want to go to jail if something happens!', she said laughing.

'Be here tonight, it's already late!', Sunita said seriously.

'OK, let's see', replied Narmi calmly.

Sunita now came near the bed pulling a chair and she started applying lotions on her body. Then she went on painting her lips and eye lid.

'Why? Going to party again?', asked Narmi teasingly.

'I'm doing it for you!', said Sunita and smiled fixing her eyes on Narmi.

'But it's time to bed, girl!', counter replied Narmi.

'So what? I'm a girl!', replied Sunita again.

Then there was a silence in the air. None of them talked or turned their face to each other. Sunita's voluptuousness provoked Narmi but he dare not to cross the boundary. He was fully awake and conscious, but everything in this world has a limit. He sat there, staring at Sunita, and he knew she was well aware of the moment. Sunita hesitantly stood up and went to a corner. Narmi feared she would slap him or ask to leave her room. But to his surprise she came and sat near Narmi. There was a Ponds body lotion in her hand. Opening the cap, she asked in a rather nervous voice.

'Can you help me apply this on my back Narmi?'

'It's out of my reach!', said she in a low hesitant voice.

'Ah, yes! Why not?', replied Narmi taking the lotion from her hand.

With a trembling hand Narmi started smearing the lotion over her body. His hands moved slowly and carefully as if he was giving a final touch to a portrait. Narmi began feeling the warmth of her body and almost forgot himself. He was experiencing a change in his body mechanism which he couldn't explain in words. Sunita now loosened her wrapped towel and said in a shaky voice.

'Won't you go down stupid!'

That one sentence was the *beginning and end of everything*. Narmi could remain no more in the state of dormancy. His hand began moving instinctively and spontaneously. He first gave a big hug and she didn't complain. Narmi pulled down Sunita on the bed and began exploring her body.

'Put off the lights Narmi, please. Please Narmi', she whispered taking a deep breath.

Narmi started kissing Sunita on her lips and she equally responded. He then slowly moved his lips down her neck and unlashed the knot of her bra. He then started feeling the contours of her round, smooth and puffy breast. He squeezed them till Sunita cried out. Her nipples grew taut and Narmi started running his tongue. Out of excitement she pinched Narmi's back and ran her nails around his body. Narmi could hear her heart thumping so close and paid a deaf ear to the happenings outside! Her lips were luscious, but Narmi was not yet satisfied. He wanted to explore more and wanted to discover the unknown. He moved his hand around her waist and slowly pulled down her flowery undergarments from her smooth thighs and finally kicked them off into the air.

'You scoundrel! Trying to loot my treasure?', whispered Sunita tickling Narmi in the armpit.

She then kissed Narmi even more passionately and smiled. This arouses and excites Narmi till he became irresistible. Guiding her hand to his undergarment, Narmi whispered with a tremble.

'Pull it down, please! Please Sunita. Would you?', he asked repeatedly and she did accordingly.

Nothing could stop Narmi now! He began to take his time.

'Oh, it hurts Narmi. It's painful!', said she breathing heavily.

They started moving tandem in a rhythm. Sunita cried but Narmi had no time to listen. It lasted at least for half an hour and when everything came to a halt, Sunita said.

'This is my first time!'

'Really? Are you serious?', asked Narmi putting his head on Sunita's bosom.

'I'm a virgin. Oh, no! I was a virgin', she cried pulling Narmi's ear apart.

'I'm sorry! I won't repeat! I won't repeat!', begged Narmi laughing.

Sunita hugged Narmi lovingly moving her fingers around and asked after remaining silent for a minute.

'Narmi, what about you? Do you have a girlfriend?'

'I'm a virgin too!', answered Narmi with a sigh and added, 'You're my first!'

'Is it? Really?', asked Sunita in a whisper.

'Yes, I promise!'

Sunita pulled Narmi by her side and kissed him on the forehead. They lay there on the cot together and Narmi for the time being found himself in the seventh heaven under Sunita's arm. They never knew how long it was going to last but it was a beautiful and wonderful beginning, deep and intense. As days rolled, they met almost every day and enjoyed sex whenever they got the opportunity. Narmi would meet his desire of lust in Sunita whenever he needed.

After a month of their relationship, Narmi missed many of his friends. Yajum, Hidam, Sanjay and Tujum grew quite indifferent to him and mocked him giving a title 'Fevicol', which meant adhesive.

Aware of his approaching exams, Narmi wore a worried face one day while walking along the stone pavement towards Ganga with Sunita.

'' What's up Narmi? '', '' You look quite tense today? '', asked Sunita staring at Narmi.

'' Nothing '', '' just…''

'Our exams are very near', replied Narmi in a low voice.

'And so you've created this face of yours; because of exams or do you fear missing me?', asked Sunita in a jesting tone.

'Let's get serious now!', 'would you?', asked Narmi.

'Yes, but what if I didn't see you?', echoed Sunita.

'Don't worry. I'm not seeing another girl!', replied Narmi.

'That's why I love you! So, so much indeed!', said Sunita pulling Narmi's palm.

'I think I should leave…', said Narmi casually looking at Sunita reaching Ganga.

'Leave me? Leave me huh?', cried Sunita. 'Even without…'

Sunita turned away without a word almost in tears and Narmi had to follow and console her.

'I…I, didn't mean that way! You are so childish man!', said Narmi giving a hug.

The hug got its intensity and electrified Narmi's animosity and he started kissing her passionately which ultimately ended with a blasting sex. Narmi absentmindedly made a pillow of Sunita's fluffy boops and looking towards the ceiling said, taking heavy breath.

'I think we ought to be serious now!', 'It's high time', he added.

Sunita seeing Narmi worried, didn't put any comment. She got up from the bed and went inside the kitchen to see if there is something to eat.

'Yes, we should be wise and act like matured person!', said Sunita casually while putting the plates.

After the lunch Narmi had to take leave of Sunita. She has become quite serious for they won't be seeing each other during the exams. Sunita followed Narmi to Ganga bus stop, seeing him off with a heavy heart.

'I shall visit you after few days', said Narmi in order to console Sunita.

The college exam lasted for about a month and Narmi had to burn midnight oil throughout. He was aware and conscious and listened to his inner voice. He avoided his friends and even forgot Sunita for the time being; except Atai who would visit him occasionally. They together would spend hours at IG Park studying beneath the shade of pine trees. Remaining far from the chaos they would find solace in the nature's lap.

On the last day of the exam, Narmi felt like a bird freed from a cage. He felt a big burden thrown out from his back. He started looking for his friends and wanted some kind of fun and recreation. He met Yajum, Hidam and Tujum who were happy; burden being thrown off.

'Let's celebrate!', cried Tujum throwing a book of history in the air.

'Oh. yea!', cheered Yajum.

'Where is Sunita?', asked Hidam in a jeering manner which made her friends to laugh.

'Where is she? I really mean it, Mr. Fevicol', added Yajum.

Narmi's face almost turned red under the blazing sun feeling nervous. This made his friends to make fun of him. But they were real good friends. Those remarks didn't bring any change in the way of their friendship. Then accidentally, Narmi noticed Sunita and Atai coming in their direction. He felt a real inner solace seeing Sunita who was his beloved now.

'Where did you go stupid? I was looking everywhere for you!', cried Sunita seeing Narmi.

'I was here only, expecting you', replied Narmi cheered up.

'Beat him up! Sunita', said Tujum smiling.

'Finally over!', cried Sanjay joining the group.

'Let's have something in the canteen', proposed Taniang.

'I'll pay! I wrote my exam well', he added.

Narmi had a refreshing chilled cola and samosa with his friends at the college canteen. Left alone, he walked back to Ganga with Sunita. They were there, chatting on various topics. Narmi was eager to have a long discussion about the recently concluded exam while Sunita was curious to know where and how Narmi was planning to spend the break. She was also worried that she would be missing Narmi during the college break, and may be permanently in the rest of her life. She knew that she belonged to a conservative family who would never agree to such relationship. Narmi, on the other hand never gave a serious thought to though he loved Sunita.

One beautiful Saturday morning, a month after the degree exam, the university results were out. Narmi and Atai rushed to Bank Tinali to check The Arunachal Times. Narmi grabbed one and rolled his eyes to the column superscribed 'DNGC Results Out'. The boys then went through the displayed roll numbers and were much joyed to locate them. Narmi feeling exicted almost gave a big jump which made Atai laugh at his monkey like business.

'But I couldn't locate 542, Sunita's roll!', said Narmi worried.

'Let's re-check!', said Atai firmly turning to Narmi but couldn't locate the roll 542.

'May be she got stucked', added Atai and while patting Narmi on the shoulder said again.

'Now don't trouble yourself, we will check in the college!'

Narmi and Atai then hurried down to 'C 'sector and revealed their happy news to Neyang who was back from office for lunch.

'Mem..our results are out! We have been promoted to the 2nd year', said Atai smiling broadly.

'Is it? It's a great news indeed!', said Neyang smiling back to the boys.

'Let me see the paper', asked Tarak, Narmi's brother-in-law.

'I think we need to celebrate this happy moment', said Neyang looking at her husband who was busy reading the local daily.

That evening Tarak bought a big fat hen from Gandhi market to celebrate Narmi's pass result. Mrs. Yarek who was invited that evening appreciated Narmi vehemently and said.

'Keep up this! You're the true *Boum Kakir* of this modern time'

'You must not try to imitate the rich boys. Be determined!', Mrs Yarek added.

After the wholesome meal Narmi lay down on the cot beside Nai, looking up with his legs crossed and arms akimbo. His mind wondered from one point to another restlessly. Sometimes he would think about Sunita and sometimes about his future. Whenever he closed his eyes he had the picture of Sunita and in subconscious state, sometimes he would bable to himself. Somewhere Narmi had the feeling that he was responsible for Sunita's failure. So he decided not to continue the relation even if she turns up after the college break.

After two weeks the college reopened and Narmi was a bit excited hoping at the scope of meeting his friends and may be, Sunita if he was fortunate enough.

'Hey, how do you do?', asked Tujum seeing Narmi.

'Fine, thank you!', replied Narmi with a smile.

'Long time no see!', said Yajum who was with a bunch of old friends.

'Where is S?', asked Hidam with her brow raised.

'No news!', replied Narmi quietly and went towards library with Atai.

That afternoon Narmi and Atai went to Ganga to check if Sunita had come. The boys were shocked to see that the rented room previously occupied by Sunita was now occupied by a Bihari family. Narmi wondered and got astounded at Sunita's unfeelingness. He thought she should have informed him atleast. Atai knowing the situation didn't talk much and picked up different topics to divert Narmi's mind. But Narmi was happy for one thing that from now on he would be able to give more time to his studies. Narmi loved Sunita, but she was like a gust of wind that passed through his window, a mirage in the desert and a short lived hallucination.

<hr>

Narmi passed the rest two years without Sunita or without a Sunita. Though a bitter feeling of emptiness haunted him for a long time he was able kick his ass off finally. Narmi did his Bachelor of Arts with honours in English literature. Neyang was the happiest sister on earth at the moment when Narmi came smiling with his degree result and Nai was very hopeful that one day his brother would be recognized and given a place in society.

'Oh, what should we do?', said Neyang looking at her husband.

'I think we must celebrate this happy moment!', she said again.

'My brother is a graduate in English now! It's a huge achievement', she breathed with relief.

Tarak nodded half-heartedly but had no intention to displease his wife's interest. Narmi on the other hand didn't mind such ruly behavior from his brother-in-law, as he knew Tarak as a class twelve fail student. On the other hand, Neyang always celebrated Narmi's success and she has always been a constant source of inspiration for the boy. That night they had a little party without much item on the menu.

'I 'd have taken more if I had an extra belly', said Tajing hiccupping after the wholesome meal which made Neyang laugh at his peculiar remarks.

'So what's your plan Narmi?', asked Tajing who worked as Lower Division Clerk at Secretariat.

Narmi remained quiet for sometime but came up with a reply. His mind was already occupied with various thoughts. He spoke with hesitation.

'I feel like doing PG at Arunachal University'

'That's great! English has a lot of scope', said Tajing with a lot of support.

Neyang who was expecting her third child smiled and looked at her husband Tarak. Nai seated at a corner, was busy playing with his nephew Kaling. Tarak after a while made a casual remark:

'Eh, B.A. is enough! Getting a job is more important'

'That's true. But do you think Narmi should be a LDC like me?, 'asked Tajing.

'I'm 45, a father of two, yet we are scolded by young officers', added Tajing.

Neyang and Nai laughed looking at Tajing but Tarak was silent. It seemed he felt a sort of realization of what he had said. Nodding his head he said again.

'Of course, that's true!'

'Then?', Tajing gestured raising his eye brows and looking at Tarak.

'Join PG Narmi. Always be industrious. One day you will get your reward!', advised Tajing.

'I'm there *Babing*, don't worry!', said Nai with a smile.

'That should be the spirit! Why would you stop him when he is…'

Tajing didn't complete the sentence. But it was understood. Even Nai, who was a fifth standard fail could understand without much pressure on his head. That night Narmi had a sound sleep. He was full of gratitude for Tajing who was just an old acquaintance, but with so much of moral support. Narmi was now determined to step into yet another milestones of his academic ambitions. The mere thought of Arunachal University would bring smile on his face.

CHAPTER SEVEN
RONO HILLS

Rono Hills, where Arunachal University lay, a place as quiet as heaven, cool and serene; far from the cry of the city was a perfect place to realize his dreams Narmi thought. Though he had never been to, he kept his ears open to hear various comments about this place. Standing thoughtful outside their government quarter at C' sector, he fancied about the University. Sometimes he would look around and somewhere on the orange horizon, would see imaginary visuals; of grown up men and women walking here and there with books and notes in hand. Other than medical or engineering, it was a place where top brains from different academic backgrounds gathered. Narmi longed for this place despite financial constraints. He knew his Neyang would support no more as she was already burdened with three growing up children. His only hope was his little brother Nai, who fortunately was still a bachelor.

'I want to see my brother on the top, your success is my success', Nai would say often.

But his dreams loomed like a mirage along the unknown horizon, distant and unseen unless he set out and work. So, few weeks later Narmi and Tujum had decided to visit Rono Hills in order to make enquiry about the various courses the University offered. The most unfortunate thing that happened to them on the day was that they missed the university bus as soon as they reached Nirjuli shortcut.

'O, damn it man! The bus's gone', Tujum sighed looking at Narmi.

'We will find another', said Narmi hopefully.

The university bus sped away leaving behind Narmi and Tujum. Narmi stood there on the stone pavement rubbing his eyes briskly because of the smokes thrown by the bus. He felt miserable inside but was trying to cover them by remaining calm.

'We get there by any means!', he said after sometime feeling desperate.

Tujum already appeared tired and hopeless and sat beside Narmi crouching. He was picking up pebbles and throwing them here and there in order to pass his time. Crossing Dikrong suspension bridge they found a truck carrying pebbles to a construction site at Rono Hills. Finding no other means Narmi and Tujum had to board the truck and reached the university. Narmi had a sigh of relief in the evening as he was able to collect prospectus from the university office. Narmi excitedly went through the leaves of prospectus and decided to do his masters in English Literature. He never knew whether he was giving justice to his aesthetics but it was his personal choice.

So in a few days Narmi became a university student. He along with Atai and Tujum started attending classes at the university. Narmi had always been a sincere, punctual and hardworking boy and this was known to many of his close friends. It was during his PG days that Narmi met this girl Jomgam who later became his life partner. Narmi still remember, they had an unromantic beginning. After all at PG level when one is tangled in the hectic schedule of paper works and studies, scope of romantic episode is almost void.

'This's my friend…Narmi', introduced Tujum to Jomgam one day at the university canteen.

'He is…future lecturer!', added Tujum patting Narmi's shoulder.

'Oh, don't make such insensible joke man!', broke in Narmi smiling shyly looking around.

'Oh is it?', said Jomgam smiling back to the boys.

For Narmi it was just a casual meeting. He never thought things would turn different and go deep. They started seeing each other every day at the university library and sometimes at the canteen. Thus they became good friends and within a year became lovers. But Narmi had a different experience now with Jomgam. His need for Jomgam was not bodily desperation but a need to sustain life. He ultimately needed a partner to share his feelings of joy and sadness and this fair skinned girl had this in her. For Jomgam too, Tujum's single sentence explanation about Narmi at their first meeting was enough to woo her heart. Moreover a girl with sensible heart would never deny a boy like Narmi unless they hunt for money. Narmi spoke less and had a gentle and reserved personality. He attended his classes regularly with deep involvement. He had been an intense observer and listener. He watched Mr. Roy, Associate Professor in the English department at the university. Though short and bald headed, he was popular among the university teachers for his flawless English and eloquent lectures. Girls were almost crazy for this middle aged man from Calcutta. His verbosity and use of ornamental language would easily impress even a layman if they happen to be in his class. Narmi observed him with intense attention and watch him with great curiosity during the delivery of his lecture. He wanted to be like him though he had never spoken to any of his friends. So he started preparing for National Eligibility Test for lecturership even before his PG. Though he worked very hard, his two NET exams didn't bear him any fruit. Nevertheless he didn't lose his heart and kept working thinking that one day or the other he would achieve his goal. For Jomgam, she was always on Narmi's side and she too believed that one day Narmi would surely get through the exam. For Narmi it was not just the Roy lectures, but college and university teachers were almost the post where nepotism couldn't influence. Furthermore he loved Rono Hills' atmosphere where one gets so much space for the growth of mind.

In June after two years, Narmi completed his PG. He had a very satisfying smile when he found himself among the top ten lists in the university result. Neyang and Nai were equally happy at the brother's performance. They had a bigger family party this time. Narmi though excited was half hearted too, knowing the fact that he needed a job to support himself. Neyang the godmother was now quite hopeful that he would get himself engaged somewhere with such a vast knowledge, that he had gained from his university studies. Narmi on the other hand kept himself very busy and led a very hectic life. Routine studies, checking the daily newspapers and keeping the account of happenings around him became his every day task.

One day Narmi and Atai returned from IG Park after spending sometime in the open atmosphere. Narmi looked tired and exhausted. Atai kept himself busy with Neyang's youngest son Kayin who was just three years old.

'Atai..! long time no see. How are you?', asked Neyang returning from her office.

'Fine Mem', 'I just returned from my village yesterday', replied Atai with a broad smile revealing his dimple.

Though Atai smiled the hollow indexes of his reflection told that he too was passing through the trauma of unemployment and non-engagement. Educated youths sitting idle near ponds and throwing pebbles were a common sight of the day.

'Don't panic. As you sow, so shall you reap', said Neyang looking at the boys.

'It's only three months after your PG', 'I'm sure a job is waiting for both of you', said Neyang in a didactic tone and went inside the room.

'Boys here are some refreshing tea for you. Come!', said Neyang with a tea tray.

The boys enjoyed the hot ginger tea and later Atai had to depart as evening had already fallen. Narmi had a hard night that evening. His mind roamed between Jomgam and then his present situation of being unemployed. He loved Jomgam immensely though she belonged to *Galo tribe* but marriage was something that would't come easily unless he got engaged somewhere.

One day, as usual while Narmi was turning the pages of Arunachal Times, his eyes caught the sight of a small box of advertisement in an insignificant corner where it was written; WANTED ENGLISH TEACHER @ 3000 per month. Narmi didn't believe his eyes; his heart began to beat faster than usual and at once he began decorating his certificates. They were the biggest asset for him, so he took outmost care and loved them more than anything else. On the appointed day Narmi rushed towards VKV Itanagar. The walk-in-interview was held in the principal's office. Narmi was a bit shocked to see so many candidates even for a single post of a teacher. He remembered the words of his friend's mother, *'Don't throw stones, it would hit a graduate'*.

But sitting there in queue for sometime, he regained his confidence and entered the chamber boldly when his name was called.

'Why M.A.?', asked the first interviewer, an old man with a bald head. Isn't graduation enough?

'Quest to know more and discover myself. An arts graduate is almost insecure and immature!'.

'Good!', said a man sitting at a corner.

'Why do you want to be a teacher?', asked the man seated at the centre.

'Teaching is not an easy profession and teachers have to face many challenges. But it's the only job where you feel that you have done something good for the society'.

After putting few more questions the board released Narmi. Though he answered most of the questions Narmi was not satisfied with his performance. So he lazily waddled back to C' sector following the short cut through IG Park.

The result was declared the next day. Narmi was selected. The principal informed him through a phone call. Narmi almost gave a jump out of excitement and at once called Jomgam.

'I'm fine. Thank you. After so many days?'

'Yes, I have been busy', Narmi replied.

'I thought you have forgotten me!'

'How could I? I'm not a Casanova!'

'Who knows what goes behind the curtain!'

'Anyway leave that and come to the point. I have a bad news!'

'What? What happened? Anything wrong?'

'I got selected as a teacher in VKV'

'Wow! That's a wonderful news!'

'Now I can introduce you to my family!', added Narmi after Jomgam got quiet.

'Nervous?', asked Narmi.

'…a little bit but a bit excited!', replied Jomgam shyly.

'Anyway I'm coming down to Doimukh to pick you up on Sunday'.

'Okay, that's fine'

'Okay, I take your leave now. See you soon, bye'

'bye', said Jomgam and left the phone.

One day on a specified Sunday, Narmi called Jomgam and introduced her to his few family members. It was none of a formal meeting like a Punjabi or a Bihari does. Marriages are simple among tribals. If a tribal opposite sex move together openly and sleep in the same bed they are considered a married couple. It was a happy family meeting. Neyeng gave a broad smile as ever, seeing the 'would be' daughter-in-law for the first time. Nai, calm and composed sat in the corner of the sitting room and Tarak raised sorts of formal questions to which Jomgam answered shyly.

That evening Narmi and Jomgam slept in the same bed under the knowledge of the family members and thus they became an acknowledged husband and wife. Narmi had now become more alert and laborious being a responsible man. He had been working for the last six months at a very meagre salary at VKV, when one day he saw an advertisement in The Arunachal Times demanding a lecturer in English. Narmi once again decorated his certificates and at once sent the attested photocopies to principal, Arsang College at Pasighat, headquarters of East siang district, some odd 300 kilometers from the Capital Itanagar.

CHAPTER EIGHT

BACK TO PASIGHAT

On the appointed day Narmi attended the viva-voce at Pasighat and surprisingly made through it. He was back in Pasighat almost after a decade. His old hostel reminiscence would haunt him and he was quite happy to be back in the town where he spent his childhood.

Being selected as lecturer in a college affiliated to a central university Narmi was a content man now. He was on half-way to his final destination. Jomgam swelled with pride at Narmi's achievement. On the day of his joining, he met the other new recruits, Miss Pema, Miss Henter, Miss Manju and Kanu who later became his close friends. Dr. Gagam, the principal welcomed the new members to his college. Seated comfortably in his arm chair he spoke in rather throaty voice.

'Good morning my friends, welcome to Arsang college'

Rolling his eye balls anti-clockwise and again adjusting his spect with the tip of his fore finger, he began.

'So you are Narmi from English department, you are Pema from History, Henter from Political Science, Manju Hindi and Kanu from Economics department'

'I hope I'm right?', he asked pushing his spect up again.

All smiled.

'I'm Dr. Gagam, your principal. I'm from Pasighat'

'Arsang is a newly established college run by a trust. It aims to bring better and quality education especially in our Siang district'

'Be sincere, dedicated and give your best output'

'We need to attract more and more students. You see, government colleges are over crowded', he added and laughed to himself.

Then he pressed the calling bell and a boy of around 15 rushed in. He stood before the principal almost in attention position, bending his head low. Every one laughed.

'This is my boy!'

'Migom, bring in the tea and sweets for our new members'

'He is a very smart boy', said Dr. Gagam again and laughed.

The new members saw each other and laughed again. After tea, Kanu shook hands with the girls and made queries about their whereabouts. He was a bit excited seeing the girls and having the idea that he would be working with those girls in the same college.

'See you girls', he said waving his hand and took his leave from Narmi too.

Narmi took a room near Solung Ground and attended his duties without fail. He loved his work and worked with full dedication. After six months of teaching in the college, he brought Jomgam to Pasighat who now was working as Lower Division Clerk in a government department. Narmi being a male chauvinist prig suffered a defeat as his wife was earning better than him though he is a lecturer. He would often become gloomy and get lost in thought.

Jomgam would recognize his frustration at many crucial hours and tried to encourage Narmi in many ways.

'You have got ample time Narmi'

'Believe in yourself, one day you will achieve your goal', Jomgam would say.

One afternoon while Narmi and Jomgam was sipping tea in the veranda, the rent owner, a widow in her sixties asked Narmi.

'You are in which office son?'

'I teach in a college', replied Narmi quietly.

'Lecturer! Oh, I mean officer rank?'

'Not exactly'

Narmi and Jomgam looked at each other and laughed.

'How much you are paid?', the old woman asked innocently with eagerness.

'This much!', replied Jomgam loudly displaying her five fingers.

'Wow!', 'Fifty thousand? 'said the old woman and finally left with a heavy sigh.

When the woman left Narmi and Jomgam rushed into the room and burst into a feat of uncontrollable laughter. Thus they were a very happy couple in terms of relationship. They were almost envied by their friends.

'Best couple', marked Ejum, one of Jomgam's office staff.

Narmi had been working for two and a half year when his frustration was taking a permanent shape. Though he was preparing hard he almost found it impossible to get through the eligibility test.

Unless he does that he was sure, he would not be able to fulfill his dream of teaching in a university or a college. His constant efforts fail to bear the fruit that he had been expecting for long. In a way he was very staunch in his decision. He never looked for other jobs neither fancied them. He never thought of teaching children in schools who would often purt and pollute the atmosphere. Neither, he thought of teaching high school boys, who would not respect a teacher and who would easily draw an argument.

But he was tired of drawing 5000 per month at the venture college. So he started looking for other options. Once he attended a Sarva Shiksha Abhyan Teacher, walk-in-interview at Ruksin where he met many of his friends from his village. Talen, Tarung, Takop and Yani were already there with their files. There were also many unemployed graduate youths from Ruksin, Ngorlung, Debing, Oyan and Sille.

'Why? What's up?...a lecturer attending SSA assistant teachers' interview?', said Talen almost shocked seeing Narmi.

'You will make us unemployed!', added Tarung walking towards Narmi.

'SSA teachers are better! Do you know how much we are paid?', asked Narmi shaking hands with his friends whom he was seeing after a long gap.

'Of course that may be true!', responded Yani with a serious note.

For Narmi it was something suicidal and near humiliation. A college teacher attending SSA assistant teachers' interview was something that Narmi would not digest easily. But after all, money matters! Narmi thought.

'Where is Tadam?', Narmi asked Talen looking around whom he had not met for a long time.

'He is in Itanagar, doing a course in computer', replied Takop.

The walk-in was in progress at the Extra Assistant Commissioner's office. Graduates flocked around in thousands with their certificates decorated in files. But the most interesting thing that Narni and his friends over heard was that the posts were already reserved.

'It has already been distributed among the MLAs and ZPMs', said a boy in a group standing few meters away.

'Two post are reserved for the DC', said the other.

Young candidates could be seen every where around the EAC office. Some were seen standing in group, many perched in small groups like vultures as if going to have a feast. Yet many were seen sitting alone with books and others loitering here and there. Whenever an interviewee comes out after disappearing for few minutes in the interview chamber, boys would rush and enquire what was asked by the board members.

Takom a young graduate from Debing village came out angrily from the interview chamber and almost shouted.

'This in non-sensical', 'They are doing it just for the name shake!'

'Do you know what they ask?', he asked looking around.

'Which is the capital of Arunachal Pradesh? Who is the present chief minister?'

'You hails from which village?', 'Is it a question to be asked in an interview?'

'Hopeless! I think we should resort to gun!', said the boy again and sped away in his bike.

There was silence in the air for few minutes. Narmi thought he might be yet another frustrated soul like him. People stopped talking and gazed at each other. But after sometime, the murmur resumed like the drone of bees. Narmi also thought of leaving without facing the interview but he realized that he had come a long way covering 37 kilometers from Pasighat. Finally he was called. His was 98th candidate to be interviewed.

Narmi answered all the queries put by the board. He was given some grammatical questions based on narration and voice, followed by some questions based on Arunachal which he answered correctly. Coming out of the chamber he was confident that he would be listed among the waiting lists if he is not selected. Bading good bye to his friends Talen and Talung, who were still there, he left for Pasighat.

'How was your interview?', asked Jomgam impatiently.

'Can't tell now!', replied Narmi struggling to pull out his shocks.

'Heard the posts have already been reserved for the MLAs', said Narmi breathing heavily.

'Eh, its ok. You will be a professor!', 'Why should you stoop down?', Jomgam said.

'Yes that's right. But nobody can foretell the future!', said Narmi taking yet another heavy sigh.

Jomgam's words were sweet and soothing. Next to his elder sister Neyang, she has always been there to support and encourage Narmi at every step. Two years had already passed and Narmi was still staggering in the same old college. Previously he was happy to be in Arsang college, but as days and years rolled his interest died because he didn't enjoy the status of a fullfledged lecturer. His many attempts to eligibility tests were also futile. His only friend at the college, Kanu who was now married, started taking tuitions in order to to make both ends meet.

After ten days Narmi and Jomgam visited the SSA office at Pasighat in order to check the result. Jomgam, who was a god fearing woman got up early and already prayed for good luck. Reaching the office Narmi curiously looked for the result. There were so many papers pasted on the notice board. At the right hand corner was the result displayed with a bold heading, **'Result of SSA A/T Interview conducted on 4th April** 'Narmi went meticulously through the list from top to bottom but he name was not there. There were 32 in the list and 10 in the waiting list. Narmi once again went through the lists with trembling hand but did not locate his name even in the group of waiting lists. When he checked the third time he was shocked to find one of his friends listed among the waiting list group. Narmi came out almost struggling as there were many boys and girls who came for the result.

'Took so much time?', said Jomgam standing beneath a tree.

'what? Have you to go some where?', asked Narmi some what in a loud voice.

'It's crowded inside!', said Narmi sweating all over.

Jomgam understood. She need not be taught. She has been with Narmi for almost four years now. She could recognize his every mood and movements. His taste, desires and weaknesses were not something new to Jomgam.

'Lets go', said Narmi and Jomgam followed quietly.

Jomgam did not say a word and walked side by side sharing the umbrella. It was a hot sunny day and they almost got their skin burnt under the hot sun. After walking for some time Narmi spoke out when they were nearing BSNL office.

'I thought it was a mere gossip', said Narmi.

'What?', asked Jomgam curiously.

'Tadam is in the waiting list'

'So?', asked Jomgam again looking at Narmi.

'He was in Itanagar on the day of the interview!', said Narmi.

'You mean?'

'Fool, he was absent. He didn't attend any interview!'

'Why then he got listed among the waiting list?', asked Jomgam angrily.

'God only knows!', replied Narmi.

'Lets go and complain', said Jomgam with a tone of frustration.

'What can we do? Moreover he is our friend'

'These things do happen', said Narmi.

'Then why not with you?', asked Jomgam in bad temper.

Narmi had no answer to this question when he is engrossed with unsolveable questions of life. So he simply laughed pulling Jomgam to his side.

'Let's have some sweet', Jomgam pleaded and they disappeared into the crowded Siang Bakery.

That night Narmi couldn't sleep well. He wanted to cry but he realized that he was a man after all. His mind wandered from one thought to another. He then thought of his colleagues who were highly educated. Miss Pema was pursuing her PhD and Henter armed with an M Phil degree. These thoughts helped him to restore peace in him and accept the situation where he was. He attended his duties well and had a good rapport with everyone.

One day when Narmi arrived at the college, Pema and Henter appeared very excited. When questioned, Henter handed over a newspaper that was in her hand. Narmi went through the paper and found out the secrets of their smiles.

'Oh, advertisement?'

'So you are leaving us very soon!', added Narmi staring at the girls.

'Oh, Oh,…no!', 'Don't count the chicks before it hatches!', cried Pema.

A minute later Kanu and Manju also joined the table. After their classes they sat together again. The principal, Dr. Gagam was in good mood. He picked up many different topics and issues and shared extended lectures on them. He was a sort of an orator that engulfed every listener. Dr. Gagam also knew about the advertisement. He advised.

'You must go for other better options too'

'For me its ok, as I'm a trustee member', he added and got up to leave.

In the following month Pema and Henter were selected as Assistant Professors. Miss Pema was posted at Bomdila College and Henter at Dera Natung College at Itanagar. The faculty members of the college along with the principal had a small party hosted in favour of the out going Lecturers. While congratulating Pema and Henter, he said.

'I'm happy that you have been selected but it's a great loss to Arsang College', said he and smiled.

Then with a change of tone he said looking around.

'Nature give time for every season. You should be patient and hopeful'

'There is no substitute to hard work. Confidence is yet another ingredient of success in life', he added while concluding his speech.

When the party was over Narmi, Kanu and Manju shook hands with Pema and Henter. It was yet another blowing moment for

Narmi which aggravated the pain inside him. A kind of fear started gripping him from top to bottom. It was Jomgam who consoled him from time to time.

That evening Narmi and Jomgam went to the terrace of the building to enjoy the cold wind blowing since it was hot inside the living room. They spread a carpet and lay on their back looking at the million stars above. Narmi didn't say much as his mind was already occupied with various thoughts. Jomgam had collected a bottle of chilled beer and served Narmi who started sipping them slowly. The mixture of chilled beer and temperature drop, because of the wind were a perfect combination for Narmi's soul to remain at peace. It made him forget everything and prepared him for a sound nap. So Narmi had an occasional drink whenever situation demanded.

The resignation of Pema and Henter created a hollow among the staffs and to the two departments of History and Political Science. Lecturers had to be brought from JN College to fill up the gaping. Now in order to take temporary refuge, Narmi joined B. Ed. course though he never intended to become a school teacher.

A year after the completion of B. Ed, Narmi had a surprise call from his elder sister Neyang. She informed him of an advertisement that had appeared in the Arunachal Times demanding for the posts of Senior Teacher in English. Narmi gave a big jump and told Jomgam who equally reacted. But Narmi remembered Miss Pema's word and said.

'Do not count the chicks before it hatches'

'Why? This time you must do it or you never do!', warned Jomgam.

'Let's see what happens!', replied Narmi quietly.

'Go to Itanagar within this week to drop your application form', Jomgam insisted.

'I leave day after tomorrow', said Narmi.

Winning or losing was not a question now. Narmi was happy beyond measure even at the mention of the advertisement. He had longed for it and his patience was at stake. But Narmi was worried at the same time because of the SSA interview tragedy. He was quite aware of the happenings around him but he remembered Shakespeare's famous line.

'Cowards die many times before their deaths ;

'The valiant never taste of death but once'

'Why should I run away without facing the battle?'

'Either I do it or I die!', murmured Narmi to himself.

That was it. Narmi was determined to give his best effort. The question of winning and losing didn't bother him anymore. He left the God to decide that. He was confident but surely not over confident. He recalled the lines of **Walter D Wintle**, which he once read.

> *If you think you are beaten, you are*
> *If you think you dare not, you don't.*
> *If you'd like to win, but think you can't*
> *It's almost certain you won't.*
>
> *If you think you'll lose, you're lost,*
> *For out in this world we find*
> *Success begins with a fellow's will;*
> *It's all in the state of mind.*
>
> *If you think you're outclassed, you are;*
> *You've got to think high to rise,*
> *You've got to be sure of yourself,*
> *Before you can ever win a prize.*

Life's battles don't always go
To the stronger or faster man;
But sooner or later the man who wins
Is the one who thinks he can.

On the day specified he attended the interview. His coming was a big occasion for Neyang and Tarak. Narmi's nephews, Kaling and Kayin and nieces Ponung and Yamum were the most excited after seeing their uncle after a long gap. Nai, the younger brother was very happy at his brother's arrival. They welcomed Narmi as if he was a hero. But he stayed there only for a brief period as he was working in a private college. This saddened Neyang and her kids.

One day as Narmi was doing *'The Unknown Citizen'*, by W.H. Auden to the students of B. A. 2nd year he had a surprise call from his sister.

'Narmi, you are third in the list', said Neyang very excitedly.

'Third! What third?', asked Narmi innocently.

The result was delayed three and a half month. Narmi had almost forgotten about the interview. One day while he was turning the pages of The Arunachal Times, he saw a letter in the *Readers' Forum* which demanded early declaration of ST interview result. Having read that he gave up his hope and accepted his fate.

'Stupid, you have been selected', said Neyang giving stress.

'I…I, mean the results are out?', asked Narmi to confirm.

'When? Today?', added Narmi still confused.

'Yes! The paper is with me!', cried Neyang.

'Oh, my god! Thank you so much', breathed Narmi at last.

'You have been posted to Tuting, Upper Siang District'

'Your brother-in-law went to the office today!', added Neyang.

Narmi wouldn't believe till then. His heart started beating fast and he could hear his own beat even without a statoscope. He rushed out of the college immediately without telling the principal and his friends. He felt restless, and wanted to reach his rented house as soon as possible. He was overwhelmed with excitement, and wanted to share that moment of happiness with his wife Jomgam. So he broadened his steps and hurried towards Solung Ground. People stared at him, but he didn't care and left them behind. When he reached, Jomgam was already there, back from the office. He rushed into the room, caught hold of Jomgam and gave her a big hug.

'Oh, my god! What's up?'

'Why this hug?', asked Jomgam laughing loudly.

'I…, I…ultimately made it!', said Narmi in a trembling.

'Is it dear?', asked Jomgam excitedly.

'Yes, it's in today's paper!', said Narmi still gasping.

Jomgam freed her hands from Narmi's clutch at once. She turned aside and wept with tears of joy. Narmi had no strength left to resist his emotion and followed Jomgam. It was a moment to be celebrated, a moment to be cherished and a moment to be remembered. Narmi and Jomgam celebrated this success in a small but in a very charming way. They went to the market together, got a bottle of chilled beer and plates of *Chow mein*. Went to the terrace of the building, spread a carpet, lay on their backs. The night was clear with millions of stars shinning above. The *spoon stars* could be seen easily. Narmi had a sip of chilled beer and when he was not sipping he talked. Jomgam was happy and excited but not satisfied. She felt a kind of tightening in her throat. She got up, called her parents at Doimukh and revealed Narmi's selection. They were equally happy and congratulated Narmi immensely. Thus she started pressing from one number to another. She also called her old friend Pema, who has now earned a PhD degree.

'Narmi, here's a call for you', said Jomgam hurrying towards Narmi.

'Who's it?', asked Narmi.

'Don't ask, just pick up!', Jomgam persisted.

'Yes, hello!', said Narmi.

'Cogratulations, finally you made it, Narmi!', said the voice.

Narmi at once recognized the voice. It was Pema who left Arsang two and a half years back.

'Thank you, but…. you know what I actually wanted to be!', said Narmi in a hesitant voice.

'I know', said Dr. Pema.

'Be satisfied with what you have got!', advised Dr. Pema.

'*A bird in hand is better than two in the bush*', added Dr. Pema.

'There are many who see big dreams, chase them but who fails to grab them!', said Dr. Pema in a didactic tone.

'Do you know what I wanted to be?', asked Dr. Pema again.

Narmi was quiet and listened like a good boy as Dr. Pema spoke.

'I wanted to be an IAS officer',

'But I couldn't clear even the state civil service!', said Dr. Pema in a grave manner.

'God has given us different roles and responsibilities and we need to accept them!', she added.

'You have the freedom to dream and chase them. If you grab, it's ok. If not, accept the other course!'.

Having said that Dr. Pema bade *'good night'* to Narmi and left the phone. Narmi was there, calm and composed, gazing at the million stars above. Jomgam, who lay by his side didn't say a word. On one occasion a shooting star was seen far south leaving behind trails of light, but they didn't react. Narmi's mind wandered from one thought to another. Sometimes little reminiscence of childhood would haunt him but then they were interrupted by the present moment. He thought about his days at CWC and BKMS. Then he started thinking about DNGC, and about Sunita who had disappeared from his life like dusts in the wind. There was no coherence in the way of his thought. They shifted in a haphazard manner. He also fantasized about his dream of becoming a college or a university professor and of the consequent failures. But he gave a big frown and smiled to himself, thinking about the present moment. Jomgam was already asleep, but to him night was still young and full of hope. Finally feeling exhausted, Narmi went into a long deep sleep. When he woke up, Jomgam appeared with a cup of tea. Smiling she said, *'good morning darling!'*, and they had a beautiful day ahead...